FETCH!

Geraldine McCaughrean

Activities by
Esmonde Banks and **Laura Russell**

ALWAYS LEARNING

PEARSON

Published by Pearson Education Limited, Edinburgh Gate,
Harlow, Essex, CM20 2JE.

www.pearsonschoolsandfecolleges.co.uk

Play text © Geraldine McCaughrean 2013
Typeset by Phoenix Photosetting, Chatham, Kent, UK
Cover design by Miriam Sturdee
Cover photo/illustration © Pearson Education Limited
Activities text © Pearson Education Limited 2013

The right of Geraldine McCaughrean to be identified as author of this work has been
asserted by her in accordance with the Copyright, Designs and Patents Act 1988.

First published 2013

16 15 14 13
11 10 9 8 7 6 5 4 3 2 1

British Library Cataloguing in Publication Data
A catalogue record for this book is available from the British Library

ISBN 9780435149420

Printed and bound in China (CTPS/01)

Contents

Introduction

I remember museum trips with school – that air of wariness which said, 'We're on an outing; there's a picnic lunch. There's got to be a catch.' And there was, of course: some question sheet to fill in, and written work back at school: *My Trip to the Museum.*

But the things that stuck in *my* mind were never the ones on the question sheet. They were the stuffed tiger seal, the camel bridle or the chariot from a Somerset bog; or the elephant painted by a man who had never seen an elephant.

The Head of the British Museum was asked to reveal his favourite exhibit in the whole place. He brought out Kozo – a great pine-cone of a dog with a head at each end; a cartoon of a dog, with iron nails instead of fur; a push-me-pull-you of a dog. One hundred, two hundred years ago, it ran messages for its owners.

My first thought was 'Want one!' My second was to wonder what messages Kozo was asked to carry. And how did the Kongolese tribespeople *picture* the wooden dog's to-ing and fro-ing? Hardly Timmy the Dog with a note tucked in his collar. Hardly Lassie – 'What's that, Lassie? Someone's fallen down the well?!' No. Because these were messages driven home with a hammer and nails. These messages were between the Living and the Not-Alive.

I like dogs: there is a funny mixture of protection and helplessness about them. Mine can depend on me for food; I can depend on her for love. (She would open the door to a burglar, but no dog's perfect.) Every society has an interesting relationship with its dogs. But not many would think of driving nails into them.

The big emotions are pretty much the same from continent to continent, from age to age, from birth to death. Fear, sorrow, jealousy, longing – these lie in ambush for all of us, and when they strike, nothing short of magic can rescue us. So these are the kinds of things (I decided) that Kozo would be asked to carry between worlds.

If a modern-day Kozo turned up on eBay, who would bid for it? Thousands, of course, for a laugh. Perhaps even you, for a laugh. But plenty would bid in deadly earnest, I'm sure, straining to reach into the forests of the Past or the orchards of the Future; yearning for answers ... even though, in their heart of hearts, they know that hurts aren't mended with a hammer and nails.

Cast list

Main characters

Rochenda, *sensible, responsible and intelligent but in despair because of her mother's recent death*

Kelly, *her best friend, protective of her*

Minnie, *Rochenda's little sister, of infant school age*

Liam, *like Rochenda, except that his grief comes from his mother expecting a new child by a stepfather he hates*

Whitman, *his reaction to everything is to make a joke of it, but underneath the jokes, he has good sense and is sensitive to Rochenda's unhappiness*

Colly, *has a sceptical attitude to the things that get other people excited*

Ajax ⎫ *have their heads full of zombie and action movies and*
Grogs ⎭ *are fascinated by the horrible; they are also fairly dense*

Anorax, *clever, with a wealth of knowledge, mostly gained from the Internet*

Obi, *clever and into music*

Jojo, *young, naïve, sentimental to the point of soppiness*

Filly, *a friend of Rochenda's who likes to be a part of things even if she is not quite sure what is going on*

Harry, *asks questions, usually short and to the point*

The visitors

Nganga Juam Parfait Mapity, *a Kongo nganga (witchdoctor) who, since his death, has become not only educated but wise*

Mayifa, *his wife, fierce, scary and permanently angry; she behaves like a witch, and is fiercely proud of her husband*

Jomaphie, *a Kongo tribeswoman, cultured and well spoken*

Mudashimwa, *a Kongo tribesman and amateur psychologist*

Cherubin, *a Kongo tribesman, gentle and chatty*

Museum staff

The Curator, *loves history, loves his museum, but is less at home with the children who visit it.*

Staging suggestions

The way that any director or cast approaches staging a play is bound to be only one way of looking at the text. Even the oldest plays are endlessly reinterpreted as we continue to find new ways of looking at them. Quite simply, there is no right or wrong way to stage a piece, but there are ways which offer greater or lesser challenges to actors and audiences. These staging suggestions will depend more on developing a strong ensemble feel within your cast than they will on bulky and costly sets. As a theatre-goer, I feel the drama starts to die the moment a curtain closes and we hear the scenery trundling around, and it can take a long time to regain lost momentum. I always want the story and the characters to keep moving. I think audiences are happy to suspend disbelief and use their own imaginations if you reward them with a performance that has wit, charm, style and vision, even if you are working in a limited or limiting space.

Fetch is about very complex ideas and emotions, not places and spaces. We need the audience to be able to really pay attention to how the characters are feeling, so make sure you pay attention to the pace and rhythm of the piece. The play has a real pace to it but make sure you leave space occasionally for the audience to reflect on the expressions and gestures of the characters.

The locations which need to be defined in *Fetch* are as follows:

- Museum
- Rochenda's Bedroom
- School

These need to be created with minimum fuss to help the story along. The vast majority of the play takes place in Rochenda's bedroom so don't waste much time and energy on the other spaces particularly when the bedroom holds some special challenges of its own.

Costumes

This play takes place in two distinct worlds; the contemporary urban world and the historical, rural Kongolese world. There are lots of young people in this piece with very different personalities so, try to use some distinctive visual signifiers to help the audience quickly discern who is who. A scarf, an anorak, a baseball cap or a pair of big headphones will help those watching to navigate through the many characters.

The look of 'the visitors' needs to reflect their time and place – some time spent researching Kongolese culture and history will furnish you with suggestions.

Light & Sound

Use a natural lighting state for the museum, bedroom and school, they are very much part of our world. Consider bringing in some sound (traffic, murmuring people) to reinforce these spaces.

When we see the visitors, everything changes – suggest the otherworldliness of these people through lighting with coloured gels and gobos. Also consider placing lights in unusual places to throw odd shadows. Back this up with the sounds of insects, animals and music from central/west Africa and any audience will know it is somewhere entirely different.

Transitions

Use the space between each scene to remind us of the distinctly strange world we are delving into. A hint of lights and sound which reflect 'the visitors' will give us the sense that they are close at hand if not visible.

Think about having music as the audience enter, during the interval and as the performing space empties which reflects the apparitions too. Create a whole experience for those watching which starts before the play begins.

Challenges (the visitors, the animals)

This play gives your actors and audience the chance to learn about the Kongolese people, their culture and beliefs but could have you tying yourself in knots working out the right approach. Don't panic about cultural sensitivities, but do examine them. No one expects the actor playing Hamlet to be Dutch or Macbeth to sound Scottish, and remember that all drama is pretence. I think the text, costumes, lights and sound will give any audience all they need to know, the dialogue suggests an archaic manner of speech so I don't think your actors will need to affect a Kongolese accent that will most likely be inaccurate.

The animals are something you need to make a clear and consistent decision about. Real dogs, rabbits, birds and tortoises are scene-stealers and come with attendant-possible-chaos. Toy or puppet animals tend to have a comic quality on first sight but may prove easier to rehearse and perform with.

Scenes
Museum (scenes 1.1, 1.4)
Rochenda's Bedroom (Scenes 1.2, 1.6, 1.7, 1.8, 1.10, 2.1, 2.2)
School (1.3, 1.5, 1.9)

When staging *Fetch*, I would suggest that your approach is very impressionistic about the Museum and School and very detailed about Rochenda's bedroom.

A simple plinth and a sign (or a small and mobile stage-flat) will suffice for the Museum, everything else can be suggested by the cast.

The School need only have the sound of a bell if you think you need it. Some blocks or boxes set about the place will give characters something to sit, lie, or stand on to create some interesting shapes. The truth is, that the audience don't much care if this is a school, park or town centre – what the cast are saying is much more important than where they are saying it. Don't waste resources on making the school feel like a school.

Pour your energies into making Rochenda's bedroom work. It needs to feel normal and natural yet also large enough to hold lots of characters. A practical, workable door and window, as well as bed, drawers, chair, wardrobe etc. will make it feel solid and real but we also need it to be *invaded by apparitions*. One striking way of achieving this would be to cover stage flats with cloth which has vertical slits cut into it – this would mean that the ghosts can literally walk through the walls which should create a memorable image.

Rochenda's room will not be the kind of set which can be created or 'struck' quickly or simply, so I suggest that your production utilise three performing areas. Perhaps place the Bedroom centrally and the Museum and School either side – or even in three different places in your auditorium/studio. Not only does this make for a dynamic visual experience for the audience (just gazing at one spot can be wearing) but it also helps keep the pace up. The action follows Rochenda and if she can simply step out of one space and straight into another there is no loss of momentum. It is a joy to watch a piece with no scene-changes, just be careful that light doesn't spill too much.

I hope these suggestions solve, rather than create, problems. They are intended to give your cast as much responsibility as possible. They aim to give your pupils a sense of the contemporary ensemble theatre-making which is widely used by companies like Complicité, Kneehigh and Improbable and will develop their performance skills rather than relying on expensive trickery.

Richard Conlon

For Ade

Act One

Scene 1

Exhibit.

*A school outing is visiting the British Museum.
The curator is struggling to raise any enthusiasm
for his exhibits.*

COLLY: *(Bored silly)* Oo look. More **artefacts**. They
should have people in museums. People
would liven the place up.

GROGS: Not if they were dead. And stuffed.

AJAX: They got dead people. They got mummies   5
in the basement.

JOJO: Oo I wouldn't like to see mummies. They
must smell horrible.

WHITMAN: Their breath doesn't smell at all.

HARRY: Just get this place. Looks like Camden   10
Market. Colourful or what?

CURATOR: We come now to a later phase in the
continent's history …

FILLY: We're still in Africa, right?

WHITMAN: Going to be a long ride home.   15

COLLY: How'd they get hold of all this stuff?

CURATOR: The African section, yes, but moving into the
19th century.

HARRY: S'pose people give it in here when they don't
need it.   20

KELLY: *(To Rochenda)* You all right, girl?

ROCHENDA: Yeah. Yes. I'm all right.

HARRY: Like, you buy stuff on holiday 'cos it's outstanding, right. Like a hat for instance. Then you get it home and think 'What am I going to do with it?' Can't go out and about with it, can you? Get arrested. 25

COLLY: *(Reading a label)* **Assagai**.

WHITMAN: 'ats-a-guy. 'ats-a-gal, Coll. You'll learn the difference when you're older. 30

GROGS: Could you do the business with this, sir? I mean, could it kill something?

AJAX: Not much point in a spear if it won't kill anything.

CURATOR: Actually, that one was probably only ever used **ceremonially**. Look at the care that's gone into making it. There would have been more workaday spears made for hunting. 35

GROGS: But would it kill a man?

ROCHENDA: Why would you want to? 40

JOJO: Don't know: revenge, maybe? If he'd killed my husband … Or my **terrapins**.

COLLY: Who'd want to hunt your terrapins with a spear?

WHITMAN: Pixies? 45

COLLY: Assagai. It's not a spear, it's an assagai. It says.

HARRY: *(Seeing the **nkisi**)* Oh I like the dog. The dog I like.

CURATOR: Yes. He's rather fine, don't you think. This is Kozo. He's a nkisi – that's to say a sacred 50

artefact carved by the Kongo people native
to an area approximately that of present-day …

HARRY: Why the two heads?

WHITMAN: *(Whispering)* It's a **cut and shut**. Two 55
dogs – both rear-ended in a pile-up on the
M4. They welded the two doggy wrecks
together.

CURATOR: The Kongo is an ancient tribal culture dating
back many hundreds of years. They buried 60
their dead in the woods, far from the village.
Superstition made them afraid to go there.
Their dogs, of course, roamed around freely,
as dogs will. They hunted in the woods, ran
about among the graves … An idea grew 65
up of the dog as a creature able to travel
between the Living and the Dead.

ROCHENDA: *(The words jolt a reaction)* What?

CURATOR: Developing on that idea, Kozo here is a
messenger dog. This head points towards 70
the future – the Dead, the Afterlife.
Whereas this end points the opposite way
– towards the spirit world of those yet to
be born …

LIAM: *(the words jolt a reaction)* What? 75

CURATOR: … or reborn, of course, if you think of life as
a cycle of birth, life, death and **reincarnation**.

AJAX: You mean this dog could carry messages to
the dead?

CURATOR: Yes. Well, after a fashion. In a manner 80
of speaking.

FILLY: You could make a wish, and your dead relations would …

CURATOR: Not exactly.

OBI: It's hammered together with rusty nails! 85

CURATOR: Not quite. Every time a member of the Kongo wished to make connection with the spirit world – for help, say, or good fortune or to settle some unfinished business – they would visit the local 'wise man' – the 90 **nganga**—

GROGS: Witch doctor, you mean.

CURATOR: Nganga. And he would hammer nails into the carving – driving home the point, as it were. Oils, herbs and **essences** were burned 95 on the nkisi's back during the ritual; note how the wood is charred and stained … Kozo is a go-between between worlds, you might say … No, please – don't touch. This particular nkisi is only 100 years old, but it 100 is fragile nevertheless. It has come a long way, after all. There is at least one split in the wood, look.

HARRY: I'd split if someone hammered nails into me.

CURATOR: Exactly. 105

GROGS: Could it fetch bodies back from the dead – zombies, like?

CURATOR: Definitely not. That idea would have been horrific to the Kongo. But it was certainly credited with mystical powers. It would 110 have been held in the keeping of the nganga, as I say, and he would be a member of the Country-of-the-Dead Society.

WHITMAN: Beware of the dog, then.

CURATOR: *(On leaving the room, his **droning** voice fading*   115
to a silence) Exactly. Now if we pass through
to the next room, you will start to see the
impact of international land-grabbing and
colonisation on the economies and
independence of African nations.   120
Slavery, of course, had been making its own
impact for two centuries …

*All follow except Rochenda who deliberately
hangs back, looking **furtive**. She picks up the nkisi
like a baby.*

*A pulse of light and the chirrup of insects sweep
the room momentarily. Her friend Kelly comes back
for her.*

KELLY: What you doing?

ROCHENDA: It's nice. I like it.

KELLY: Put it down. You might break it. They'd   125
sue. Put it down, girl.

*Rochenda drops it, accidentally on purpose. The
nkisi falls in half.*

KELLY: Rochenda! What you done?! You gone and
broken it now!

ROCHENDA: It's all right. I'll take it home and mend it.

KELLY: Don't talk daft, Roche! Put it back! Prop   130
the two halves together. They'll never notice
till after we've gone.

ROCHENDA: No. Needs a drop of superglue, that's all. Be
good as new.

| KELLY: | You think they won't miss it? Great wooden dog with two heads? Where you gonna put it? | 135 |

KELLY: You think they won't miss it? Great wooden 135
dog with two heads? Where you gonna put
it?

ROCHENDA: This parka's got pockets inside. Two halves.
Hangs even, look. Doesn't it?

KELLY: What's that, then, your shop-lifting jacket? 140

ROCHENDA: *(Outraged)* I never shoplifted. What, you
think I'm a... ? I'm just going to take it home
and mend it. Then I'll bring it back ... What
do you want?

Liam has re-entered.

LIAM: Where's Kozo? 145

KELLY: Who?

LIAM: The dog; where's the dog?

ROCHENDA: Someone came and took it away. To mend
that crack.

LIAM: *(Plainly disbelieving her, but not able to reveal
his own interest)* Yeah. OK. 150
Re-enter Ajax, rounding up stragglers.

AJAX: Our coach has come back early. We have
to skip the rest of Africa.

KELLY: There is a God.

AJAX: So hurry up, right? ... Where did the dog go?

LIAM: Someone came and took it away. To mend 155
that crack.

*He and Rochenda exchange the looks of rival
conspirators. All four hurry to catch the bus.*

Scene 2

Rochenda's bedroom.

She has mended the dog with superglue. Now she sets about writing a note.

Enter her little sister Minnie who sees the dog and goes to stroke it.

ROCHENDA: Don't touch it, Minnie. Glue's not dry yet.

MINNIE: Is it ours to keep?

ROCHENDA: 'Mine', not 'ours'. No. It isn't a toy.

MINNIE: What, is he real, then? What's he called?

ROCHENDA: No, 'course he's not … it's called Kozo. It's a   5
nkisi.

MINNIE: Pink Dog wants to meet Kozo.

ROCHENDA: No, she doesn't. Don't pick it up: it'll stick to
your hands and you'll never-ever-ever be able
to put it down.   10

MINNIE: They could get married. We could have a dog
wedding. Pink Dog could marry Kozo. You
don't have to be a corgi to marry a corgi, not
if you're a dog: Charlie says so.

ROCHENDA: Pyjama-case dogs don't fancy wooden witch-   15
doctor-type dogs, though. It's a well-known
fact … What are you, a dating club for dogs,
now? … No, don't kiss it, Minnie! Your lips
will get stuck and Dad'll have to take you to
hospital and they'll have to cut your lips off   20
with a knife.

MINNIE: Kozo doesn't like all those nails sticking in him.

ROCHENDA: He's like a **fakir** dog. Fakirs sleep on beds of nails. They love it.

MINNIE: What's a fakir? 25

ROCHENDA: No idea.

MINNIE: I think Kozo's hungry.

ROCHENDA: No. Kozo's just got earache from listening to you. All right. Go and tell Pink Dog there's another dog in the house. 'Course she 30 might go mad with jealousy and come up here and bite chunks out of Kozo and probably swallow a nail and die.

Minnie is finally persuaded to go. Rochenda hears her meet Liam on the stairs and tries to hide the nkisi under some clothes and stand in front of it.

LIAM: Can I come in?

ROCHENDA: What you doing here? 35

LIAM: And you have a nice day too. Just passing. Your dad said to come up. He's watching the Shopping Channel.

ROCHENDA: He does that a lot. Watch things. He's not really watching. It's just on. Passing, why? 40 Where were you going?

LIAM: *(Shrugs. Prowls about as he talks, trying not to look as if he's looking)* Just walking. You know. They're painting the nursery at home. Stinks of paint. Gives me a headache. Smells the same here. What is that smell? 45

ROCHENDA: **Chanel No 5**.

LIAM: *(Seeing the glue)* Superglue. Deadly that stuff. There was this man in our street glued his

eyelids together and they had to cut them
open and he could've lost his eye. You need   50
a licence to use that stuff.

ROCHENDA: No you don't, just a reason.

LIAM: Wouldn't mind a look at that dog.

ROCHENDA: What dog?

LIAM: That dog there. The messenger dog.   55

ROCHENDA: Didn't know you liked art.

LIAM: Didn't know you liked thieving.

ROCHENDA: I didn't thieve it! I brought it home to mend
it. I knocked it down.

LIAM: Knocked it off, more like.   60

ROCHENDA: What, you think I'm going to sell it on eBay?
One **shabby-chic**, African, two-headed dog,
as seen in the British Museum. Why would I
steal it?

LIAM: To wish on it. Something mad like that.   65
'Cos you want to—

ROCHENDA: Yeah? Say it. What?

*Liam is too embarrassed to mention Rochenda's
mother.*

*Call from offstage: 'Rochenda. This remote ... come
and show me again.'*

ROCHENDA: God! What is it with people over forty. Why
can't they cope with technology? *(Waits
unsuccessfully for Liam to go)* I'm not keeping   70
you, am I?

LIAM: I'll wait here for you.

Exit Rochenda. Liam uncovers the dog and studies it. Agitated and upset, he lifts it down on to the floor. He gets out a hammer and nail and goes to knock it into the dog's back.

Enter Minnie.

MINNIE: Stop it! Don't hurt Kozo!

LIAM: I wasn't …

MINNIE: You're mean. How would you like it? 75

LIAM: I'm mending him. He sprained his back. I'm going to make Kozo well. If you don't want to see, don't look … Just push off for one minute, Minnie, will you?

MINNIE: I'll tell. 80

LIAM: No! No, don't. Your call. But it's your fault if Kozo doesn't get well.

MINNIE: I'll tell Rochenda. And Daddy. And the woman that breaks the Hoover. Now you have to kiss him better and say you're sorry. 85

LIAM: I don't do kissing.

MINNIE: You can't be a vet then.

LIAM: I never said I was a vet.

MINNIE: Vets kiss sick things better.

He puts away his hammer, and puts the dog back on the shelf.

LIAM: Not tigers they don't. Or anacondas. Or 90
skunks. Or jellyfish. Or tarantulas.

Rochenda returns.

LIAM: Or fire ants. Or slugs. Or leopard seals.

ROCHENDA: I have to wash my hair.

MINNIE: Liam was being a vet.   95

LIAM: *(Hastily)* Show me the way out, Minnie. Your sister isn't feeling like visitors.

Liam leaves, managing to take Minnie with him before she can make any accusations. Rochenda shuts the door behind them, lifts down the dog on the floor and starts sticking pellets of folded-up messages to the dog with superglue.

ROCHENDA: Come back Mum. I can't bear it, Mum! I went up the Garden of Rest yesterday, but you weren't there. Why would you go   100
there? You never went there. I can't cope. I've tried and I can't. There's Minnie and she doesn't understand and Dad says to her, 'Mum's gone away for a little while' and how does that help? She just goes on   105
asking and asking and thinking you're coming back. He can't face it. Just sits there all day watching *Cash in the Attic* and *CBeebies*. He doesn't go to bed – just sleeps where he is, and he doesn't eat. We   110
don't eat 'cos eating feels too normal, too much like nothing's happened when we all know it has. Oh come back, Mum! I could dream you – that's how you could do it! – I could dream you and in the dream you   115
could tell me what to do, and I'd get your face fixed in my head … photos are useless. They don't look like you, not really. And you could hug me and sing 'Summertime' and cook chicken nuggets – boring, ordinary   120

stuff … Send help, Mum! It's like I'm buried
and nobody knows and everyone thinks it's
going to be all right and it isn't. 'Time's a
great healer', they say; and 'If there's
anything I can do', and look at me with   125
their big, sorry eyes and their little, sorry
mouths, and I want to say 'All right, then,
GET HER BACK. GET HER BACK! GET MY
MUM BACK! I WANT MY MUM BACK!' But
I'm not supposed to shout and carry on   130
because I mustn't upset Minnie. 'Stay brave
for Minnie,' they say, 'Be a big brave girl for
Minnie.' Come back here from wherever
you are! Tell Kozo to … I don't know …
bring you back. If he's so magic …   135

*Partly disgusted with her own foolishness, she
puts the dog on a shelf.*

ROCHENDA: Go on, then. Fetch, why don't you?

*Nothing happens. Rochenda gathers up shampoo
and towel, and exits (supposedly to the
bathroom).*

*There is a pause. Minnie opens the door and
sneaks in. She has a bag of gold chocolate coins.*

MINNIE: I brung you a chocolate. It's one of my
Christmas stocking ones. I've been saving
them for best, but you can have one.
Night-night Kozo dog.   140

*She puts it into the dog's mouth, kisses it, and
exits. A faint patter of drums. A flicker of light, as
when a gritter lorry passes.*

Scene 3

At school the next day.

ANORAX: It doesn't look African. More Roman, I would have said.

GROGS: It's definitely old.

COLLY: Might be valuable.

HARRY: And where did we find it, again? 5

KELLY: Rochenda found it in the nkisi dog's mouth this morning.

ANORAX: I'll look it up on the Internet. There's loads of coin sites.

OBI: What was she doing there? 10

KELLY: Where?

OBI: At the museum.

GROGS: She wasn't. She nicked the dog from there yesterday. To mend the crack. Apparently.

Obi and Whitman look at each other, out of their depth.

ANORAX: *(From the computer)* And it's bronze, with a 15
head on it, right?

HARRY: Maybe someone is trying to get in touch.

WHITMAN: Texting's easier.

ANORAX: *(Ticking computer boxes)* Is it knurled?

FILLY: Knurled? 20

KELLY: *(Who doesn't have a clue)* No, it's not knurled.

ANORAX: No knurling.

WHITMAN: They put that up in swimming pools. No bombing, no spitting, no knurling.

ANORAX: Is there a 'mintmark in the exergue'? 25

FILLY: Oh for pity's sake.

OBI: Which mouth was it in? Front or back?

KELLY: Does it matter?

OBI: One mouth for the Dead, one mouth for the Unborn. Remember? 30

WHITMAN: How many babies carry cash? Where would they get it?

HARRY: Maybe the dog's magic. Is that what we think?

KELLY: Yeah, right. And maybe someone in the last 100 years used it for a money box. Or just 35 maybe the coin got in there when it fell on the floor. Must be all kinds of old money lying around in a museum.

HARRY: You're right. They'd know about old coins. Rochenda should ask at the museum. 40

GROGS: What, revisit the scene of crime? They must have noticed Kozo's gone by now. They've probably got Rochenda on CCTV nicking it.

JOJO: Unless Kozo is so magic, it can be in two places at the same time. 45

They laugh at this absurd idea.

LIAM: *(Dead casual)* I'll take it if you like.

ANORAX: Well, it's either late Greek or early Roman. As far as I can see. Or possibly Hispanic. Or Egyptian.

JOJO: What's Hispanic? 50

ANORAX: No idea.

LIAM: I'll take it to the museum.

OBI: *(As an aside to Liam)* What's so important?

LIAM: Might be worth something.

OBI: Yeah. And?   55

LIAM: And important. Historically.

OBI: Right. You trying to get in with Rochenda?

LIAM: It wasn't there yesterday.

OBI: The coin?

LIAM: I looked in both mouths.   60

OBI: What for, man? So?

LIAM: So where did it come from? How did it get
there?

OBI: *(Laughing in disbelief)* You're never talking
magic, man?   65

Liam walks off.

OBI: Where you going, man? We've got French!
Liam?

Scene 4

Back at the museum.

CURATOR: Where did you get this?

LIAM: In my change.

CURATOR: Oh yes? In Waitrose, I suppose.

LIAM: No, sir.

CURATOR: No. That would have stretched **credibility**.   5
Where, then?

15

LIAM:	Tesco, sir.
CURATOR:	Tesco. *(He waits fruitlessly for a better explanation)* Well, I would need to check, but I would say it was Macedonian. Philip the Second. Father of Alexander the Great. So … 4th century BC? Quite rare. Really rather valuable.
LIAM:	It's not a fake?
CURATOR:	Not as far as I can tell.
LIAM:	And you wouldn't leave it … somewhere, then. For a joke, I mean.
CURATOR:	That would be one expensive joke. Where did you really get this?
LIAM:	It's not mine. Just someone at school. Said they got it in their change at Tesco.
CURATOR:	I think they lied. Would you like me to look after it?
LIAM:	No! I mean … it's not mine to leave. Someone might've lost it. They might come looking.
CURATOR:	You were here the other day.
LIAM:	Me, sir?
CURATOR:	Yes. With the school trip.
LIAM:	Yes, sir.
CURATOR:	So should I find any coins are missing from the display cases, I will know the **whyfor** and the who. You do understand that.
LIAM:	*(Not guiltily or panicked, just certain)* Oh you won't, sir. I really don't think you will.

CURATOR: I think I shall look after this anyway. If threatened by **numismatic** gangsters, you may tell them I am looking into its value.

LIAM: But …

CURATOR: Don't worry. I shall keep it safe. It shall be   40
returned to its rightful owner.

Exit Liam, angry and frustrated. Downstage the nkisi still stands on its shelf.

Enter Minnie to stroke it and feed it another secret, chocolate coin.

MINNIE: Night-night Kozo.

A brief thumping of drums, such as comes from a passing car radio.

Scene 5

Next morning at school.

Rochenda has just told the rest about the new gold coin she found in Kozo's mouth.

AJAX: Another one?!

GROGS: *(Decidedly)* Definitely a magic dog.

HARRY: Ah come on.

JOJO: Maybe it just likes Rochenda.

COLLY: And maybe Rochenda's just having a laugh,   5
right?

KELLY: She's not! She's not. She was really upset coming to school.

ROCHENDA:	I'm not saying it's … But it wasn't there last night. It just wasn't. There was nothing in the dog's mouth. 10
AJAX:	Definitely magic.
ROCHENDA:	And look at it! It's old. It's really old.
COLLY:	*(Jeering)* Left over from last year's holiday, I bet. Foreign money. Where d'you go last summer holidays, Roche? 15
ROCHENDA:	What, while my Mum was dying? Hospital, mostly.
KELLY:	You're a dork , Colly.
ANORAX:	*(From the computer)* This woman – would you say she was 'draped, wearing a crown of corn ears and a long plait behind'? 20
JOJO:	Pretty!
FILLY:	*(Looking at the coin)* Well. Yes. Sort of. Yes.
ANORAX:	Holding a long torch on the other side, with a **cornucopia** on the left? 25
FILLY:	There's a cream horn thing with stuff spilling out, right?
ANORAX:	In that case it's a gold Aureus, struck under Claudius (41 to 45 AD). I don't know where it gets us, but that's what it is. 30
LIAM:	I'm not taking this one back to the museum. He'll think I'm a coin thief.
HARRY:	Or a **forger**. He could think you were a forger.
LIAM:	I'd sooner be neither, right? 35
FILLY:	Let's all make wishes. That's what we should do. We should all go round Rochenda's place and wish on the dog.

ANORAX:	It doesn't do wishes. The curator said. It carries messages, not wishes. 40
FILLY:	OK. Well, let's send messages, then.
HARRY:	Who to?
GROGS:	To the DEAD, of course.
AJAX:	I don't know anyone dead.
OBI:	'Course you do. Boudicca. Queen Elizabeth. 45
AJAX:	Oh, right!
ANORAX:	Julius Caesar. Einstein. Leonardo da Vinci.
OBI:	Ghengis Khan. Moses. Toot-and-come-in …
AJAX:	Jack Sparrow?
SEVERAL:	No, Ajax. 50
AJAX:	Tarzan , then.
SEVERAL:	No.
AJAX:	Lara Croft!
SEVERAL:	NO, AJAX!
AJAX:	How come Obi can have Ghengis Khan and 55 I can't have anyone I want?
OBI:	I never said I wanted Ghengis Khan. I just said he was dead.
AJAX:	But why—
ANORAX:	Because your ones weren't ever actually 60 alive. They're made up. They don't really exist.
JOJO:	They don't?

19

Scene 6

Rochenda's bedroom.

KELLY:	Everyone gets a piece of paper to write their message on.
JOJO:	Everyone has to read theirs out before they stick it on, right?
HARRY:	Sellotape? 5
ROCHENDA:	The superglue's gone solid. Someone left the cap off.
GROGS:	Deadly, that stuff. I heard of a man who went to the toilet and—
JOJO:	We really do not want to know that, Grogs. 10
FILLY:	Anyone got a pen?
ANORAX:	This is mad. More coins is what we want.
COLLY:	OK. I've got a 50p. 50ps look want-able, don't they?
WHITMAN:	Not as want-able as a £2 coin. 15
COLLY:	Yeah, but I don't have £2. Not to spend on a **voodoo** experiment.
ANORAX:	It's nothing to do with voodoo.
HARRY:	I just want to cut the dog open and see if there's any more Roman ones inside. 20
ANORAX:	It's not a piggy bank. It's a nkisi.
COLLY:	Not very 'magicky', is it: Sellotape?
WHITMAN:	What did you have in mind: the still-beating heart of a magician's rabbit?
GROGS:	Now you're talking! 25

COLY: *(Contemptuously)* A hammer and a six-inch nail. Sellotape! Huh.

KELLY: Kozo's fragile. He has to be treated gently. He's a very old dog, aren't you, Kozo? … Anyway. It's only for a laugh. 30

LIAM: We should put stuff on top of its back. That's what the museum man said. Oils and herbs and stuff. To make the magic work.

COLY: The what?

AJAX: *(Liam has been exposed)* You were *listening*? 35 Liam was *listening* on the school outing, look! I never listen to people like that! It's just yackety yackety 1851 yackety yackety on the banks of the Koomyboomy … Turns my brain to concrete. Don't know why they 40 think it's educational: people telling you things. *(Derisively)* And look, Liam's got a leaflet! He actually went to the museum shop and got a leaflet!

LIAM: Picked it up when I went back with the coin. 45

KELLY: Well, you're not lighting a fire in Rochenda's bedroom. Her father would go mental.

ROCHENDA: I don't mind.

KELLY: You what?

JOJO: I think everyone's taking this a bit too 50 seriously.

WHITMAN: Yes. Lighten up, Rochenda. It's only life and death.

ROCHENDA: I've got a **joss stick** we could use.

FILLY: They turn me up those things. Smell worse 55 than Glade.

They light a joss stick and stick it into the nkisi's back. They begin to write and stick on their notes.

AJAX: Lady Godiva. Wish you were here.

HARRY: Oh that I like. Lady Godiva I like.

FILLY: Ay! Can I ask Nero if he really burned down Rome? 60

ANORAX: As long as you can write it in Latin.

COLLY: That's a point. Come to that, how's Kozo going to know where to go if we don't write everything in Kozoese?

ANORAX: Kongolese. 65

JOJO: Dogs can't read.

ANORAX: I rest my case.

LIAM: Oh get on with it, will you!

GROGS: I'm sending mine to Marilyn Monroe. Ask if she was murdered. 70

KELLY: Maybe she won't know. Maybe she just woke up dead and it was a big surprise.

JOJO: Who's Marilyn Monroe?

HARRY: Do we have to ask a question? Can't we just send a message? 75

WHITMAN: What, 'Get Well Soon'?

HARRY: I don't know. 'Reggae Rocks!' 'Tinie Tempah's the Best.'

AJAX: Tinie Tempah isn't dead, is he? Ah, he isn't, is he?! 80

REST: No.

AJAX: You're an idiot, Harry. Why d'you want to go telling us Tinie Tempah's dead?

ANORAX:	Tina Turner is.
HARRY:	No she isn't. You're thinking Whitney Houston.
JOJO:	Who's Tina Turner?
AJAX:	Nearly give me a heart attack, saying that about Tinie.
WHITMAN:	We could've written to you, then.
JOJO:	I'm doing my cat Poppy. She got run over.
WHITMAN:	Before that, did she write a lot of letters?
OBI:	What have you written, Liam?
LIAM:	That's my business.
KELLY:	No. You have to say. That's the deal. Everyone has to read out what they put. Read it out, Liam.
LIAM:	Get off! *(Screws up his note)*
OBI:	It's just a laugh, Liam. It's not for real, you know?
LIAM:	I know. It's rubbish. Sellotape. *(To turn attention from himself)* Look. Rochenda's doing hers. She hasn't read out hers.
KELLY:	Go on. What's it say, Roche? *(She reads it over Rochenda's shoulder)* 'I wish no one had to die. Ever.'
ANORAX:	It doesn't do wishes.
KELLY:	Shut up, Anorax.
ANORAX:	Sorry, Roche. Forgot.
KELLY:	How can you forget something like that?
JOJO:	Something like what?

85

90

95

100

105

110

23

FILLY:	*(Whispers)* Rochenda's mum. Last term. Died.
	Enter Minnie.
MINNIE:	Why are you sticking things on Kozo? Are they feathers? He doesn't like it. Do you, Kozo? No, he doesn't like it. 115
GROGS:	What about Conan the Destroyer. Is he dead?
FILLY:	Mine's a crossword. My gran loved doing crosswords. I thought I'd send a crossword.
JOJO:	Ah, that's really sweet! She'll like that.
HARRY:	Now what? Is that it? 120
KELLY:	I don't know. I s'pose.
	There's a general shuffling towards the door as the visitors leave one by one.
AJAX:	How quick do you think they get there, our messages?
WHITMAN:	Depends what stamp you put on.
KELLY:	Liam hasn't done his yet. Where did he go? 125
ROCHENDA:	I don't know.
KELLY:	He's dead moody these days.
ROCHENDA:	It's the step-dad thing. They don't get on.
KELLY:	Oh. I didn't know. Poor old Liam.
WHITMAN:	You'll forward any mail we get, will you, Rochenda? 130
ROCHENDA:	You don't have to be funny all the time, you know?
WHITMAN:	Beats taking a bath with an electric eel.

Scene 7

Rochenda's bedroom.

No sooner have all but Rochenda gone than Liam comes back.

ROCHENDA: You back?

LIAM: I want to send a message.

ROCHENDA: Well, you can't. You missed your chance.

LIAM: I'll tell your dad you've been smoking.

ROCHENDA: But I haven't. 5

LIAM: And that's why you lit the joss stick. To hide the smell.

ROCHENDA: *(Unimpressed)* He knows I like joss sticks. He knows I hate cigarettes.

Liam pulls out a handful of cigarette butts and tosses them around the floor.

What's with you? You want to blackmail me 10
with a handful of cigarette butts from your
dad's ashtray? Don't put ash on my bed, idiot.
You're crazed, you are.

LIAM: He's not my dad. I want to send a message.

ROCHENDA: Anyway, Dad wouldn't notice if I was 15
smoking big fat cigars.

LIAM: I want to send a message.

ROCHENDA: I heard. All right.

LIAM: In private.

ROCHENDA: Remind me: whose house are we in? 20

He holds his ground.

ROCHENDA: Two minutes. And don't damage the dog,
right? You ever try and blackmail me again
and I'll push your ciggies up your nose and
light them. Idiot.

Exit Rochenda.

*Liam takes out a hammer and nail and starts
hammering the nail into the dog.*

LIAM: Stay away, you hear? Keep away! You're not   25
wanted, right? We don't want you. I don't
want you. You'll be sorry if you come! He
doesn't give a monkey's about you. He's not
fussed. He won't stay around anyway. He'll
be gone soon. You want to be wanted? You   30
find some other family. We don't want you.
I'm warning you: I'll leave you on a bus – or
out in the snow – first chance I get. I'll put
you in the dustbin. You stay away. Mum and
I, we don't need you. Stay right away, right?   35
Don't get born, right? Don't get born. Don't
you EVER get born!

*He gets up, opens the door and finds Rochenda
and Minnie there.*

LIAM: Were you listening?

ROCHENDA: No. 'Course not.

Exit Liam.

ROCHENDA: Liam, wait …   40

MINNIE: I don't like him. He banged Kozo with
a hammer.

ROCHENDA:	Liam's all right.
MINNIE:	No he isn't.
ROCHENDA:	No. You're right. He's not. Do you want to give Kozo a cuddle? Make him feel better?
MINNIE:	*(cadging)* I'd give him a sweetie, but I don't have any.
ROCHENDA:	There's a bag of pick 'n' mix in the kitchen cupboard.

45

50

Exit Minnie.

Rochenda picks up Kozo, rocks it for a moment like a baby, and puts it back on the shelf.

Minnie comes back.

MINNIE:	He talked to the wrong end, anyway. He's stupid.
ROCHENDA:	Why? Which end did he talk to?
MINNIE:	Everyone else talked to this end.
ROCHENDA:	How can you tell the difference?

55

She strips off all the messages except one (hers).

ROCHENDA:	Kozo's beautiful, isn't he Minnie? In a hideous kind of way.
MINNIE:	No.
ROCHENDA:	No?
MINNIE:	No. He's beautiful in a beautiful kind of way.
ROCHENDA:	Ah. Do you want to watch an Aardman? Then it's bath time.

60

Exit Minnie and Rochenda.

Scene 8

Rochenda's bedroom.

The lights go down. The curtains billow. The venetian blinds rattle as if someone has left a window open. The daylight dies.

Rochenda returns in night clothes, turns off her bedside lamp and settles down to sleep. There is a noise of insects and birds.

It gets too warm. She gets up and opens the window, and goes back to bed.

Out of the wardrobe, through the door, through the window and from under the bed come the figures of grown men and women who proceed to search the room in silence. Rochenda watches them in blind terror, peeping out from under the duvet.

There is a quiet sound of drumming. They open drawers, go through the bookcase, upturn boxes, sniff the air, but say nothing. Eventually they leave the way they came, though not necessarily each by the same route as they arrived.

Scene 9

At school the following morning.

Rochenda has just recounted what happened.

COLLY: You dreamed it.

ROCHENDA: No.

FILLY: You did. You did.

GROGS: I always dream zombies after I've been
watching *The Slime*.   5

ROCHENDA: I didn't dream it. I swear.

KELLY: Does she look as if she dreamed it?

*Anorax and Whitman hold a private conversation
aside.*

ANORAX: She just wants attention. People who get
deranged by an upset like a death do that.
First she steals the dog. Now it's ghosts.   10

WHITMAN: Seeing a ghost could make you a bit
deranged, too, don't you think? ... But, I see
what you mean.

They rejoin the group.

GROGS: Ghosts would be cool. I wish they'd come in
my bedroom!   15

ROCHENDA: They weren't cool. They were terrifying.
They searched my room! Didn't you hear
what I was saying? They searched my room!
... Where's Liam?

FILLY: Why would they search your room?   20

AJAX: Drugs.

GROGS: Pirate DVDs. There's a **SWAT** team now, you
know? They raid places if they think there's
going to be pirate DVDs.

ROCHENDA: They weren't police, they were ... people.   25
In robes and bare feet and **loincloths** and ...

WHITMAN: Black, you mean. Unlike the police.

AJAX: I know a black policeman. I know two ... no,
three black policemen and that's just in—

HARRY: Don't start, Ajax.

ROCHENDA: Where's Liam?

FILLY: He's not coming in. His mother was rushed to hospital last night. Something to do with the baby.

While the others continue their discussion about the police, Rochenda moves aside to phone Liam on her mobile. (Enter Liam stage front as if at the hospital answering the call. He is in a frantic state.)

ROCHENDA: What happened, Liam? How's your Mum?

LIAM: I don't know! They won't say! Complications. That's all they keep saying: 'Complications.' What's that mean? They won't let us see her. She's in intensive care. What'm I going to do, Roche? It's my fault! It's all my fault!

ROCHENDA: No, Liam. Listen. It isn't your fault, Liam. How could it be your fault? You didn't poison her, did you? You didn't hit her?

LIAM: No!

ROCHENDA: So it can't be your fault.

LIAM: But—

ROCHENDA: It can't be your fault. Say it. Say 'It can't be my fault.'

LIAM: You don't get it.

ROCHENDA: Yes I do. Yes I do. But you can't wish a baby to death.

LIAM: I meant for the baby not to get born – not for both of them to … I'm so stupid! I never thought of it cursing Mum!

ROCHENDA:	The dog doesn't do wishes, Liam. You said 55 yourself: the dog doesn't do wishes.
LIAM:	But I told the baby not to come, and now—
ROCHENDA:	No, you didn't. You told a lump of wood. You told a bit of tree full of nails. And you didn't burn all the right resins and herbs and 60 things, did you? And Sellotape. I mean, Sellotape! So … it's a coincidence, Liam. Calm down and think about it. It's a coincidence. Coincidences happen. Your mum will be fine. 65
LIAM:	I don't mind about the baby! I'll put up with it if Mum can just be all right!
ROCHENDA:	I know. Don't panic.
LIAM:	Should I tell them?
ROCHENDA:	Tell who? 70
LIAM:	The doctors.
ROCHENDA:	Tell them what?
LIAM:	That I cursed the baby!
ROCHENDA:	You didn't curse the baby, Liam. You just said a few things. You were upset. No. I honestly 75 don't think you need to tell the doctors. *(She looks back at the others laughing and kidding around)* They'd just laugh.

Liam rings off and exits.

The others can now be heard saying:

OBI:	The coins were real.
FILLY:	That's true.
OBI:	Hard to see really how they got there. 80

COLLY: Got where?

FILLY: Got in Kozo's mouth.

COLLY: If that's really where she found them.

ROCHENDA: You really do think I made it all up. Why would I do that, exactly? To make the dog 85 look magic?

JOJO: I believe you, Roche. I think there are ghosts. My Auntie Maureen saw a ghost once, down Etam. It was trying on leggings in the changing room. And I know there's ghosts 90 up the theatre, because they do ghost-watching nights. Be stupid to have a ghost watch if there weren't any ghosts, wouldn't it?

ROCHENDA: I don't know.

OBI: So what were these barefoot ghosts 95 looking for, do we think?

WHITMAN: Their shoes?

ROCHENDA: How would I know? The people who sent them messages?

KELLY: Their family. You know: their children's 100 children's children's children.

FILLY: What, like their descendants?

GROGS: Their way back to Deadland?

AJAX: Well, duuuuh. Their dog, obviously.

ROCHENDA: But they didn't take their dog. It was there, 105 plain to see, and all they did was look in its mouth. Mouths.

HARRY: Ah. There you go, then. They want their money back.

COLLY: What, those coins? 110

ANORAX: Oh Hades.

HARRY: Well, they looked in the dog's mouth, didn't they?

ROCHENDA: Where are they now, those coins?

OBI: One's at the museum. The curator took it off Liam. 115

ROCHENDA: Well, where's the other one? I'll give it back! I'll put it back in the dog's mouth.

All eyes turn to Anorax.

ANORAX: I sold it.

HARRY: You what? 120

ANORAX: I sold it. On the Net. I thought we could share the take.

FILLY: Oh yeah? That's why you came into school today flashing the cash and pushing fivers in our faces. 'Share the take'? 125

ANORAX: I was going to.

FILLY: Suppose the coins were sent to pay for something. Maybe. And maybe last night they came looking to collect.

AJAX: Payment for what? Like a take-away? 130

HARRY: Or something at Argos, you mean?

FILLY: I don't know, do I? No, not a take-away, idiot. Some sick person to drag off to the Underworld.

WHITMAN: A ticket to see Kongo United play at Upton Park. 135

GROGS: A vampire bride! A blood offering! A ripped-out heart!

KELLY: Shut up, Grogs.

FILLY: And now they haven't got it – whatever it is – they want their money back. 140

WHITMAN: *(Trying to be the voice of reason)* Maybe they just didn't like us taking the mick. We did take the mick out of a lot of dead people.

COLLY: *(Doubtfully)* You mean it was Marilyn Monroe and Lady Godiva? 145

ROCHENDA: They were African.

KELLY: Whitney Houston? Tinie Tempah?

WHITMAN: Oh don't start Ajax off again.

ROCHENDA: And they didn't sing. Or rap. They just searched. 150

KELLY: Maybe when Roche wished 'nobody was dead', she … you know … like brought everybody back to life.

JOJO: What, everybody? That's millions and billions! Everybody who's ever died? Come back to life? 155

COLLY: All together in Rochenda's bedroom. Mmmm. Standing room only.

OBI: In actual fact, there wouldn't be standing room on the whole planet. 160

ANORAX: Depends when you count people as starting from. I mean cavemen? Neanderthal man? The great apes?

WHITMAN: The whole planet would spin out of orbit and crumple like a leaky football. 165

GROGS: That's incredible!

ANORAX:	Also, it's not true, because there didn't used to be many people in the world. They multiplied as they went along.	170
OBI:	What, like that grains of rice on a chess board thing? One on the first square, two on the second square, four on the third—	
ANORAX:	Whatever. Anyway, there'd only be about twice as many people on Earth if everybody dead came back to life.	175
COLLY:	Talking numbers, can we divvy up the coin money now, Anorax?	
ROCHENDA:	I don't want to be in the house tonight. I'm really scared.	180
WHITMAN:	Don't be, then. We'll swap. You sleep at mine, I'll sleep at yours.	
KELLY:	*(Possessively)* You come and stay at my place, Roche.	
ROCHENDA:	No. No, I can't. I have to be home for Minnie.	185
KELLY:	She's got your dad.	
ROCHENDA:	These days that's no different from being alone. No. I have to. But I'm just so scared they'll come back.	190
WHITMAN:	Well, why don't we all come over to your place. Massive sleepover.	
JOJO:	Ah sweet! I haven't done a sleep-over for yeeears!	
FILLY:	Parents don't like it after junior school. They think we'll 'partay'.	195
JOJO:	But we'd be ghost-watching, not partying.	

AJAX: Yeah. People do ghost-watching all over. Castles. Haunted houses …

ROCHENDA: *(Desperately grateful)* Would you do that? They won't come if all of you are there.   200

JOJO: Won't your parents mind us all turning up?

KELLY: Jojo!

JOJO: What?

KELLY: Small head, big mouth.   205

ROCHENDA: Dad won't care. He doesn't care about anything any more. Please come … And if they do come, you'll know I'm not making it up.

WHITMAN: You're really not making it up, are you, Roche?   210

ROCHENDA: I'm really not. On Minnie's life.

KELLY: Or you could stay over at my place instead.

ROCHENDA: No! I can't leave Minnie on her own.

FILLY: She has her dad.   215

ROCHENDA: Like I said. I can't leave her on her own. Come about nine.

KELLY: You dreamed it though really, Roche. You must know that.

ROCHENDA: I did not dream it. I might be going mad, but I didn't dream it.   220

Scene 10

Rochenda's bedroom.

Rochenda enters. The curtains are drawn. A figure (Liam) is sitting in the dark. He lurches to his feet, wired, almost hysterical. She gives a yelp of fear.

LIAM: It's me. Liam.

ROCHENDA: What d'you think you're doing? Who let you in?

LIAM: Your dad.

ROCHENDA: Dad let you into my room?

LIAM: He told me not to break anything. I haven't   5
touched the dog. Obi rang me. Told me
about the ghost-watch.

ROCHENDA: You never told Dad it was a ghost-watch!

LIAM: What d'you take me for? … Why did you
want to go and tell the whole class? It's one   10
big joke for them. Nothing will happen with
them around.

ROCHENDA: I don't want anything to happen, Liam. I was
petrified. Can't you get how scary it was? I
wake up and every way I look there are   15
people searching my room.

LIAM: I got to see them.

ROCHENDA: You want to tell me why? *(No answer)* How's
your mum? *(No answer)* Nothing's going to
happen. Go home. You're being weird, and   20
you know the others don't do weird. They'll
never let you forget it.

LIAM: Send them home, then. You push off, too, if
you're scared. I'm not scared.

ROCHENDA: Right. You're not scared. Plainly.   25

Doorbell.

ROCHENDA: If you stay, you keep a lid on it, right? Don't blow a fuse. I say this for your own good.

Enter Anorax festooned in cameras/laptop/ thermos/stopwatch/notebook. He lays them out neatly. Meanwhile, other class members arrive with sleeping bags, pillows, sports bags, etc. Jojo has even brought her pet dog.

ANORAX: I been thinking. If we can work out how it was done – the coin thing – we can maybe suss out teletransportation , you know?   30 Time travel, even! Can you imagine how much money would be in teletransportation? If it can do coins, what's to stop us sending other things into the Past? Cures for the Black Death … And the Future could send   35 us memory sticks full of brilliant inventions!

FILLY: You brought your *dog*, Jojo?

JOJO: Daisy always sleeps on my bed. She can growl if the ghosts aren't friendly.

LIAM: What ghosts? It's rubbish. Don't know what   40 you're all doing here. None of you believes in ghosts.

HARRY: I don't get it, Rochenda. If you don't want the … shadow thingies to come again, why don't you just take Kozo back to the museum?   45

JOJO: It is a bit creepy.

LIAM:	Yeah, Rochenda. I'll take it away now, if you like. Give it a good home. RSPCA for wooden dogs, I am.
ROCHENDA:	*(Warningly)* You had any sleep lately, Liam? You look really twitched. 50
MINNIE:	You can't take Kozo away. He's MY doggie.

Whitman waits for Rochenda to put her right. When she does not, he feels obliged to say:

WHITMAN:	Kozo's only on borrow, Minnie. He will have to go back some time.
MINNIE:	What, to Hafrica? 55
OBI:	Any news on your mum yet, Liam? *(No answer. An awkwardness)*
AJAX:	What's anyone brought to eat?
JOJO:	I thought we had to eat before we came!
AJAX:	That's eating eating. I'm talking serious crisps. 60
FILLY:	I've got Ribena that's all.
HARRY:	Why?
FILLY:	It's historical. Every school trip. Every packed lunch. Every picnic. Long bus trips: Ribena Toothkind. It isn't fizzy, it doesn't make you 65 sick, and the cartons don't leak like those no-leak cup things. Parents get into these ruts; they can't break out.
COLLY:	You could always pack your own drink.
FILLY:	What, and pay for it myself? I don't mind 70 Ribena that much.
HARRY:	Colly used to bring beer.

COLLY: Only while my brother was working for
Majestic. He works for Reckitt and Coleman
now. It's mustard or nothing now … And I   75
never drank it. It tasted horrible. Any sign
yet, Rochenda?

ROCHENDA: They won't come yet. It's not dark.

OBI: I never understood why ghosts are only
supposed to turn out at midnight.   80

AJAX: At midnight, are we going to do black magic?

WHITMAN: Crisps AND chocolate.

OBI: Urch.

AJAX: And get naked?

WHITMAN: Even worse combination.   85

AJAX: They did in *Wicker Man*.

COLLY: That wasn't black magic. That was **Pagans**.

JOJO: What are Pagans?

FILLY: No good asking me: I'm **Elim Pentecostal**.
We don't hold with ghosts.   90

KELLY: What are you doing here, then?

ANORAX: I've been reading up on the Kongo. That
whole bit of Africa got sliced up by everyone
– the English, the French, the Portuguese. It
was the slavery thing. I can't imagine that,   95
can you? Turning up in someone's country
and saying, 'This is ours now; we're running
the place.' Imagine getting off the plane in
Tenerife and saying, 'Right, I'm having this
island. It's mine now.'   100

FILLY: The Turks did that in Cyprus.

COLLY: The *Greeks* did that in Cyprus, you mean.

KELLY: The Chinese are doing it in Tibet.

HARRY: We did it all over the place.

WHITMAN: We? 105

HARRY: England. The British.

ANORAX: Yes, I know. I was just saying. No one thinks that big these days.

KELLY: Except China.

WHITMAN: And America. 110

AJAX: And Russia.

OBI: Russia?

AJAX: Well, the Russians bought Chelsea, didn't they?

HARRY: And Scotland. 115

JOJO: Really? What all of it?

FILLY: My sister says Rupert Murdoch owns everything anyway. Secretly.

JOJO: Who's Rupert Morduck?

FILLY: Search me. 120

ANORAX: Can you imagine, though? People coming in the night and snatching you and bunging you on a ship.

OBI: What, like the immigration people did with Karim? 125

ANORAX: Not quite, but … they must be angry is what I'm saying. The Kongo. All those foreigners coming and dragging off their wives and children into slavery. You'd kind of want revenge, wouldn't you? 130

FILLY: And missionaries telling them they should wear more clothes and stop doing magic and stuff.

LIAM: They like putting the hex on people, too.

REST: Hey, Liam!/He speaks!/Lay it on us, man!/ 135 Thought you'd gone to sleep.

LIAM: I'm not talking Winnie the Witch here. Real witches, they only need to get the hair out your hairbrush and burn it. Anything like that. We think we're so modern with our 140 medicine 'n' wi-fi, 'n' Brian Cox on the telly knowing how the universe got started, but you still got aromatherapy, look, and lucky heather and people hacking the tusks off elephants. 145

ROCHENDA: Cool it, Liam.

KELLY: It's probably blood pressure, you know. Your mum. My mum had blood pressure when she was expecting. She was fine soon as they got her into hospital. 150

GROGS: In *Zombie Weekend*, that vicar tried to reason with them, got his arms ripped off. Matt Damon told him not to bother.

HARRY: Who said anything about zombies?

FILLY: Yeah. Give it a rest, Grogs. Real people 155 don't watch all that stuff you watch.

AJAX: I do!

WHITMAN: Two heads with but a single brain.

LIAM: They're not coming, are they? No one's coming. 160

ANORAX: You know Facebook? Well, suppose you could set up social networking with the Dead. That would have to be the invention of the squillennium , wouldn't it? We'd get so rich there wouldn't be enough money to   165 pay us. We could call it—

WHITMAN: No-Facebook. *(General hilarity)*

ANORAX: Earn a packet.

LIAM: They're not coming. I know it. I shouldn't be here. I should be at the hospital.   170

ROCHENDA: So? Go!

But Liam does not go.

JOJO: I'd want my dog back if I was them. I'd be livid if wicked white missionaries came and took my magic dog and put it in a museum. It doesn't show much respect, does it? No   175 please or thank you, just 'Give us your magic dog'.

WHITMAN: Just cold-blooded archaeology.

GROGS: Like the Toot-and-come-in man who got cursed for digging up a Pharaoh!   180

AJAX: *(With some disappointment)* He didn't get cursed. He only got tetanus or something. I saw a documentary.

OBI: Documentary? I thought you didn't like people telling you stuff.   185

AJAX: I wasn't watching. It was just on.

JOJO: It wasn't us who stole their magic dog. They can't blame us! Can they?

GROGS:	Blood feuds, they go on for generations. Like in Sicily it doesn't matter if someone's grandfather shot your grandfather; you still have to go out and shoot someone in their family. Keep it going, sort of thing. In *The Sicilian Indemnity*, Matt Damon had to kill about forty cousins and they tried to shoot Halle Berry just 'cos she was married to him.

190

195

KELLY:	Grogs, no one knows what you're talking about.
WHITMAN:	*(Gently, trying to damp down the over-excitement)* Did any of your shadows look like Matt Damon, Roche? No, so that's alright then.

200

LIAM:	They're not coming. No one's coming. Not with all this TALK. Why don't you all push off home?

205

He throws a book at the wall. There's an embarrassing pause.

ROCHENDA:	I'm tired. I didn't get any sleep last night.
JOJO:	Daisy's sleepy.
WHITMAN:	You want us to go, Roche?
ROCHENDA:	NO! No. But we should try and sleep, maybe. Minnie won't bed down till we do.

210

MINNIE:	Nope.
JOJO:	I'll take Daisy outside for a poo.
MINNIE:	Can Kozo come into bed with us?
ROCHENDA:	No. He's too spikey. You didn't bring a sleeping bag, Liam. Is that 'cos you're not staying?

215

LIAM: I'm staying.

Minnie climbs into Rochenda's bed. The rest lie down without undressing.

MINNIE: Yuck. Are you sleeping in your clothes?

Filly and Kelly go off to wash. The rest stay lying down. Filly and Kelly return.

FILLY: Her Dad's asleep in front of the telly. You think I should turn it off? They can catch   220
fire, TVs.

But Kelly is already asleep. Liam takes Kozo on to his lap, gets out a torch, and tries to remove the nail he hammered in before. Daisy the dog whimpers.

There is a noise. Liam points the torch. It lights the face of a tribesman. As before, the bedroom fills with night noises of insects and birds, shot through with piercing animal cries, rainsticks and drums. Moonlight shines despite the curtains being closed.

Whispering figures step over those sleeping on the floor. They look into rucksacks, drawers and caskets, and open the wardrobe. The tallest and most impressive (Nganga), in a long, loose robe, walks up to Liam and takes Kozo from him. Liam recoils against the wall.

LIAM: It wasn't me!

Nganga shakes Kozo, as if ritualistically, and sets it down again. One by one the class are waking up to confront what they never truly expected.

ANORAX:	*(Under his breath)* It's mass hysteria. It's not real. Crowds do it. It's mass hysteria.
OBI:	*(Hysterically)* I'm not hysterical. Do I look hysterical? 225
HARRY:	Yes.
NGANGA JUAM PARFAIT MAPITY:	Terry?
LIAM:	No?
MAYIFA:	*(Asking each in turn)* Babies? 230
CHERUBIN:	Money?
HARRY:	I'm not Terry.
COLLY:	We don't have … The money's gone!
FILLY:	WE didn't steal the dog!
AJAX:	We never! 235
KELLY:	We don't have … Somebody! What don't we have?

Panic stricken, among themselves.

OBI:	Terry who?
FILLY:	There's Terry Nicholls in Year 10.
OBI:	There's a Terry Powling at Sea Scouts. 240
KELLY:	Who'd want Terry Powling?
AJAX:	There's Teri Hatcher in *Tomorrow Never Dies*.
ANORAX:	Maybe the man at the museum's called Terry.
COLLY:	What do they want *him* for?
MAYIFA:	Terry fries! 245
KELLY:	Now I'm scared.
JOJO:	What did they say? I didn't hear!

COLLY: Terry fries! What the hell did he do?

MAYIFA: Girls. Where is girls?

JOJO: *(Choked whisper)* No! They're looking for wives! They're going to drag us off to the Underworld! Don't let them. Daisy, don't let them!

250

ROCHENDA: *(Whispers to Minnie)* Minnie, I don't want you to be scared. Listen, Min, I want you to creep downstairs and tell Dad. Fetch Dad. Don't be scared. Just wake him up. Make him come. Don't try explaining. Just make him come.

255

Minnie goes to the door. The ghosts appear to be going to block her path.

NGANGA JUAM
PARFAIT MAPITY: Are you the baby girl?

260

Liam leaps up.

LIAM: No! Don't! I take it back. Leave the baby alone! I didn't mean it! Do it to me! Don't hurt the baby! Don't hurt Mum!

*Rochenda shouts as loudly as she can 'Dad!'
Nganga reaches up, hand spread and 'catches'
the word in mid-air, cupping, then squashing it
between two hands. She shouts again. He catches
it again.*

NGANGA JUAM
PARFAIT MAPITY: Shshssh.

The children realise they are on their own, in the hands of powerful magic. General panic and sobbing break out.

ANORAX: We're not French, you know! 265

OBI: Not even descendants!

ANORAX: Nor Portuguese!

A silent pause during which Minnie leaves.

*When the Nganga speaks, it is with **serene**, perfect diction.*

NGANGA JUAM PARFAIT MAPITY: Good. My Portuguese is poor. In life I spoke only French, English and Kongolese. But the Dead are of so many nationalities: it was 270 not enough. Currently, I speak 37 languages. Shall we converse in English?

Act Two

Scene 1

Rochenda's bedroom a moment later.

ANORAX: Thirty-seven? That's impressive.

MAYIFA: *(With strident, possessive pride)* Nganga Juam Parfait Mapity is wisest man.

Minnie re-enters. She has not fetched their father; she has fetched a Pick-n-Mix bag. Most of the class are still pressed against the wall in terror.

THE SHADOWS: Revels!

The visitors pass round the bag among themselves. The light increases. The music swells again, and they dance, along with Minnie.

HARRY: What are they doing?   5

WHITMAN: They're revelling, what d'you think?

FILLY: Should we join in?

ANORAX: I never join in.

WHITMAN: I'm with you there.

The visitors sit on the floor in a circle and pass the paper bag around the circle.

LIAM: Did we summon you here?   10

MAYIFA: You? Huh!

NGANGA JUAM PARFAIT MAPITY: We should not perhaps have come uninvited, but I fear the deliciousness of the chocolate excited a great interest. It was so much envied by our neighbours …   15

JOMAPHIE: *(aside)* The Lapps especially.

MUDASHIMWA:	… that they sent us to fetch more.
NGANGA JUAM PARFAIT MAPITY:	The Terry Orange we must save, I think – though it is a temptation.
ANORAX:	So … was it you sent the coins? You aren't 20 Roman!
MUDASHIMWA:	Ah, how confusing for you!
NGANGA JUAM PARFAIT MAPITY:	There is no call for money in the Waiting Hall.
	There is a saying among the Kongo – and 25 others – 'You cannot take it with you when you go.' But the Romans, having no such saying, often arrived with coins – in their mouths – over their eyes … Hence, it is the currency most available. 30
JOMAPHIE:	I do not care much for the Romans. Such upstarts. All that they do is borrow. They even borrowed their gods from the Greeks.
MUDASHIMWA:	And so bellicose.
GROGS:	Wha's bellicose? Fat? 35
CHERUBIN:	Warlike. One brush with chocolate and they began to talk of invasion, conquest – of enlarging their empire to take in the orange orchards of Terry; taking the King of Fry hostage and having his ransom paid in 40 chocolate.
MUDASHIMWA:	Mmm. The Greeks enjoy fine food. The Romans are gobblers.
OBI:	So … Might they turn up in a minute? These warlike Romans? Looking for stuff 45 to gobble?

NGANGA JUAM PARFAIT MAPITY:	Oh no. They do not believe in the two-headed dog. Therefore the dog does not believe in them. It fetches and carries only for the Kongo. The others call our religion mumbo 50 jumbo— *(Laughs)* They asked us to bring chocolate, even so.
LIAM:	Does the dog believe in us?

The others are nervous of what Liam might say, being so wired.

ROCHENDA:	Liam, be quiet.
WHITMAN:	*(Changing the subject)* So what are you 55 waiting for, exactly? In your Waiting Hall.
CHERUBIN:	For children to be born, naturally. So we can become each like a seed in the pod, and begin another journey.
JOJO:	Ah, sweet! 60
ANORAX:	**Reincarnation**! We did reincarnation in R.E., remember?
OBI:	Hindus go in for it. So do Buddhists.
FILLY:	How d'you mean, they 'go in for it'?
OBI:	And Bob Marley. Bob Marley can get reborn 65 down my street any day he wants!
CHERUBIN:	Who?
JOMAPHIE:	That Rasta who does strange things to our hair when he's bored.
CHERUBIN:	Him? He is not Kongo. What, do they think 70 he is Kongo because he is black?

NGANGA JUAM PARFAIT MAPITY:	*(To Cherubin)* They do not understand, I think. *(To Ajax)* The Kongo Dead are reborn as Kongo children.
HARRY:	Recycling, sort of thing? 75
KELLY:	Oh Harry, honestly. The man's never going to understand 'recycling', is he?
NGANGA JUAM PARFAIT MAPITY:	On the contrary. Ecological issues are hotly debated in the Waiting Hall. After all, the future will one day be ours. 80
WHITMAN:	Please leave the world as you're hoping to find it, right?
NGANGA JUAM PARFAIT MAPITY:	Precisely. **Mots justes**. But please – please understand. This recycling has nothing to do with Hindus or Buddhists. Nor Rasta 85 musicians. We are Kongo, both living and dead. Our lives, our deaths, our rebirths are an unbroken circle. So long as we believe it will happen, it will happen. But that is the great magic in every religion, yes? Truly 90 believing that what we believe is true.
WHITMAN:	*(Quoting Peter Pan and clapping)* 'I DO believe in fairies! I do! I do!'
MAYIFA:	*(Startled)* You do?
WHITMAN:	*(Back-peddling)* Oh! No. I was only being – I 95 was only –
LIAM:	What about the messages – I mean – what I said …?

But before he can finish asking, the chief's wife interrupts with a burst of fury.

MAYIFA: This nkisi been dropped!

Silence.

MAYIFA: You hear me? Nganga's nkisi been dropped! 100

MUDASHIMWA: *(Whispered explanation to the room)* A dropped
nkisi loses its magic.

MAYIFA: This. What this on it back?

WHITMAN: *(Trying to defuse her scary rage and failing)*
Unexpected item in the burning area … Er
… It's a joss stick.   105

MAYIFA: What person do this?

*Silence. Mayifa rages round the room towering
over each one, brandishing Kozo and shouting.*

MAYIFA: You Society persons? No! Only Society
person do this thing!

NGANGA JUAM   *(Embarrassed)* Now Mayifa … My wife has
PARFAIT MAPITY: many qualities but she is no linguist. I do   110
apologise for her lamentable grammar …
She means that ceremonies should be
performed only by members of the Country-
of-the-Dead Society. It is a 'closed shop', yes?
Only **bona fide** members may perform …   115
(They are plainly not understanding him) Oh
dear. Take osteopaths! A man with a bad
back would be a fool to ask help of a
practitioner not registered with the General
Osteopathic Council … Yes? Because such   120
a man is not skilled in the art. He is likely
to make the pain worse.

LIAM: Worse?

MAYIFA:	Evil fall on him. Double evil. Double bad magic.	125
NGANGA JUAM PARFAIT MAPITY:	Mayifa – Wife – You really must make allowances for their ignorance. They meant no disrespect. Your handiwork simply fell into the hands of the uninformed.	
MAYIFA:	Has been dropped and make-mended! Who treat sacred dog this way? Pshah!	130
HARRY:	*You* made Kozo?	
MAYIFA:	Yes I make! I make for husband! I make for Nganga Juam Parfait Mapity!	
NGANGA JUAM PARFAIT MAPITY:	My wife is keenly protective of me …	135
MAYIFA:	Ai! Not to talk to them, Juam. They no respect for **orenda**!	
NGANGA JUAM PARFAIT MAPITY:	Mayifa, Mayifa, they are not Kongo! They have the orenda of their own culture.	
MAYIFA:	*(Sulkily)* Huh! Man who drop nkisi should not move from spot! Should lie on ground till the maker come and fine is paid.	140
NGANGA JUAM PARFAIT MAPITY:	*(Soothingly)* **Sois gentille**, Mayifa. How would these children possibly know such a thing? So far from our homeland? A hundred years! Four thousand miles!	145
MAYIFA:	Should lie on ground till penalty is paid!	
ROCHENDA:	Penalty?	
NGANGA JUAM PARFAIT MAPITY:	*(Slightly embarrassed)* Theoretically, after a nkisi has been dropped, if you wish to restore its magic powers …	150

WHITMAN:	… and get up off the ground …
NGANGA JUAM PARFAIT MAPITY:	… and get up off the ground … someone must pay me a goat.

Relieved laughter.

ROCHENDA:	A goat?	155
LIAM:	*(Panicky, in deadly earnest)* A goat? Where are we supposed to find a goat in Shepherd's Bush?	
MUDASHIMWA:	It sounds the ideal place.	

*Mayifa wields a rattle over each head in turn.
There's a little embarrassed laughter, but she is
scary now and getting scarier.*

MAYIFA:	*(To Jojo)* On your hands is smell of dirt.	160
JOJO:	Terrapins! I have pet terrapins! They stink!	
MAYIFA:	*(To Anorax)* On your hands is smell of money. Thief.	
MAYIFA:	*(To Whitman)* You, you have not respect for wisdom.	165

*She '**divines**' something very wrong in Liam, and
skirts round him warily, without speaking, to stand
over Rochenda.*

MAYIFA:	You, you are thief also …	
KELLY:	*(Bravely defending her friend but accidentally ratting on her)* How was Roche supposed to know any of this stuff when she dropped Kozo?	
ROCHENDA:	Oh thanks a lot, Kell.	170

55

KELLY: She tried to mend it! She did! She stuck it together with superglue!

Mayifa makes a long study of Rochenda.

MAYIFA: This one did not do breaking.

KELLY: Right! 'Cos it isn't broken, is it! The dog went back and fro with the chocolate, didn't it? 175 And the money. So it hasn't lost its magic, has it? Shows nobody dropped it. Not much, anyway.

NGANGA JUAM
PARFAIT MAPITY: It is certainly proof that someone believed.

ROCHENDA: *(Working it out)* Minnie believed. Minnie 180 believed absolutely in Kozo.

LIAM: So our messages …

CHERUBIN: Messages?

HARRY: We didn't know we shouldn't.

JOJO: We didn't hurt the dog thing. We only 185 used Sellotape.

MUDASHIMWA: Sellotape?

JOMAPHIE: *(Explaining to Mudashimwa)* For getting lion hairs off laundry.

MUDASHIMWA: Ah! 190

MAYIFA: *(Without knowing what it is)* Sellotape! Aieee!

NGANGA JUAM
PARFAIT MAPITY: May I enquire what you stuck to the nkisi with this Sellofate?

AJAX: Messages. We said.

NGANGA JUAM
PARFAIT MAPITY: Words? 195

GROGS: Well, yes, of course, words.

NGANGA JUAM PARFAIT MAPITY:	Ah! Such a delicate cargo. Picture a nkisi struggling to carry sentences between worlds. It would be like a dog trying to carry a daisy chain.

200

He looks round at blank, uncomprehending faces.

NGANGA JUAM PARFAIT MAPITY:	The things this dog once carried were too big for words. Yearning. Fear. Unhappiness. Guilt. Ambition – the kind of things we feel like blows from a hammer. You British. Always words, words. Can you use pins to hang an elephant from a tree? No more can you find words for the Big Feelings. Believe me. Not even with 37 languages. Sometimes – in my sunlit days – I would set down gunpowder before a nkisi and ignite it …

205

210

GROGS:	Wow!

NGANGA JUAM PARFAIT MAPITY:	… **concatenating** earth and air so as to wake the magic ingredients in its belly. I felt the blast myself. It stirred up magic in me, too, I promise you! (Sadly, one day it also broke my sternum and killed me, but no matter.) Now that we are dead, we *feel* the prayers spoken by the Living. We feel them like the thump of an explosion. Every day prayers rattle the windows of the Waiting Hall. The griefs. The desires. The guilty secrets …

215

220

CHERUBIN:	Fewer lately.

JOMAPHIE:	Yes. They come less often.

225

MAYIFA:	Old Ways die. No respect for Old Ways.

JOMAPHIE:	Now and then a nkisi comes loping out of the dark, bearing a message … We answer as best we can.
ROCHENDA:	HOW? 230
JOMAPHIE:	*(Startled)* In Kongolese, naturally.
CHERUBIN:	The chocolate was a pleasant surprise.
ANORAX:	You came yourselves when WE called.
MUDASHIMWA:	*(Puzzled)* No?
JOMAPHIE:	Me, I came when the chocolate called. 235

The other visitors nod in agreement.

MUDASHIMWA:	You did not summon us. We came out of curiosity and in response to your gracious gift of chocolate.
JOMAPHIE:	We were lured by chocolate. I was, anyway.
NGANGA JUAM PARFAIT MAPITY:	What manner of messages? 240
OBI:	Pardon?
NGANGA JUAM PARFAIT MAPITY:	What manner of messages did you affix to the nkisi with Sellofate?
OBI:	Ours? Oh. Stupid stuff. Stupid things. Nothing. Rubbish. We were just … you 245 know. Messing about.
ROCHENDA:	Doesn't matter. None of them got through, did they?
NGANGA JUAM PARFAIT MAPITY:	But I would be interested, even so … Were you trying to summon us? 250
ROCHENDA:	*(Agitated outburst of shouting)* NO! I didn't want YOU. I wanted …

Awkward silence.

ROCHENDA: Sorry. Look, why do you have to wait in the Waiting Hall? Why don't you just come back if you can do it. You can do it, look. You're   255 here, aren't you? People can see you! People can hear you! You can be with whoever you … want to be with! Live here instead of the Waiting Hall. Why don't you? That'd be like being alive, wouldn't it? It would be good   260 enough for me, I know that!

MAYIFA: Without flesh and blood? To be alive is to be flesh and blood!

JOJO: Eeeyoo. Gross.

MUDASHIMWA: It is all about newness.   265

CHERUBIN: All those firsts.

JOMAPHIE: Everything a surprise!

NGANGA JUAM
PARFAIT MAPITY: It is true. When my time comes to re-enter the world, I shall be sorry to lose all the understanding I have gained of my fellow   270 men …

JOMAPHIE: Except the Romans.

MUDASHIMWA: And the Australians.

MAYIFA: And Swiss.

NGANGA JUAM
PARFAIT MAPITY: True.   275

CHERUBIN: And the Nazis and the Slavers and the fashion models.

NGANGA JUAM
PARFAIT MAPITY: I must confess—

MAYIFA: And the Hatta Hittites.

NGANGA JUAM PARFAIT MAPITY: As I was saying. I shall be sorry to lose the 280
small sum of understanding I have gained
in the Waiting Hall. But it will be worth it
for the newness of being reborn.

JOMAPHIE: Every first sighting, a new wonder!

CHERUBIN: Every friend made, a triumph! 285

MUDASHIMWA: The first time you see the face of the woman
you love!

JOMAPHIE: The first time you discover that three and
three make seven!

CHERUBIN: The first sunset that ends in a green flash! 290

MUDASHIMWA: The first time a storyteller sits down at your
hearth.

NGANGA JUAM PARFAIT MAPITY: Oh yes. It will not trouble me to leave the
Waiting Hall and re-enter into life as a
know-nothing baby. Better or worse, there 295
is nothing quite like being alive!

JOJO: *(Getting carried away)* My mum's expecting!
You could come round our place! You'd like
our house. There's terrapins and two en
suites. And then you could wait in the spare 300
room till Mum goes into labour …

NGANGA JUAM PARFAIT MAPITY: A kind and hospitable offer. But to put the
soul of a Kongo into the body of a westerner
would be to put pepper into a honeycomb.
An impossibility. 305

*Liam jumps up, takes out a hammer and tries to
extract nails frenziedly from Kozo, but only
succeeds in breaking it in two. In his dismay he
howls with misery, trying to join the two
halves again.*

KELLY: I'm so sorry! He's upset. His mother's expecting. Liam, what are you like?

Mudashimwa goes over to Liam where he crouches over the dog. He takes hold of Liam's head, as if about to kill him.

REST: NO!

NGANGA JUAM
PARFAIT MAPITY: What is your diagnosis, Mudashimwa?

MUDASHIMWA: Sibling rivalry. Conflicted loyalties. **Jungian** 310
anxiety associated with fear. **Freud** might
suggest an **Oedipus complex** … but then
Freud is an idiot.

NGANGA JUAM
PARFAIT MAPITY: *(aside)* Mudashimwa has been studying
psychology in the Waiting Hall. 315

CHERUBIN: You should be happy, boy. A brother is the
best gift after a friend.

MUDASHIMWA: A sister is also good. Mostly better than a
wife. There are fewer arguments.

LIAM: I know that *now*, don't I? You think I don't 320
know that? *Now*, I know that!

Exit Liam, running from the room.

WHITMAN: His mother's ill in hospital. She might lose
the baby.

OBI: I think he thinks she's going to die.

ROCHENDA: *(Adding what no one else yet knows)* …
because he cursed the child and wished 325
it dead.

The others react with shock.

61

ROCHENDA: Liam didn't want it to get born. Doesn't like the father – his step-dad, I mean. So he wished it to stay away. Hammered a nail into Kozo, and wished. Then his mum got 330 sick. He thinks his curse is killing his mum.

OTHERS: Ruddy hell./That's heavy./Explains a lot./ What a nink.

Mayifa studies the rattle she used earlier and nods, understanding why she got such bad vibes off Liam.

ROCHENDA: So now he wants to undo it. Take it back. The curse, I mean. He wishes now he 335 never said it.

GROGS: You'd need an antidote for a thing like that. Like in *Vampire Venom*.

COLLY: Cinema's not real life, Grogs.

ANORAX: But the dog doesn't DO wishes. The man 340 at the museum said. I told you. Why does nobody listen to me? The dog doesn't DO wishes!

ROCHENDA: *(Disgusted on her own account)* The dog doesn't DO anything. Doesn't carry 345 messages. Doesn't do words. Nothing. Not for us anyway, 'cos we use Sellotape , 'cos we aren't Kongo , 'cos I dropped it. Because because because!

NGANGA JUAM
PARFAIT MAPITY: *(Trying to find out Rochenda's story too)* What 350 other messages did you send?

HARRY: Just daft stuff. Just for a laugh. Honest.

MAYIFA: Ai! No respect! No respect!

| ROCHENDA: | She never got mine. Nothing's any different from before. | 355 |

OBI: *(Strapping up Kozo with yards of Sellotape)* The museum's going to go ape when they see this. What an idiot.

| NGANGA JUAM PARFAIT MAPITY: | May I please have the answer to my question? What message did you try to send without hammer or nail or the services of a nganga? | 360 |

He confronts Rochenda, eye to eye. The chatter falls silent.

ROCHENDA: COME BACK, I SAID! I TOLD HER – COME BACK! BUT SHE NEVER HEARD ME AND SHE'S NEVER COMING BACK! I WANT MY 365 MOTHER BACK!

She hits out at him. There is nothing there to hit. She is punching air. Nganga is calmly unperturbed.

NGANGA JUAM

PARFAIT MAPITY: You miss your mother?

No answer.

Then undoubtedly she comes to you fifty times a day.

The other ghosts murmur their agreement.

| To kiss your forehead when you are sleeping. | 370 |

CHERUBIN: Pull the blanket over your shoulder.

MUDASHIMWA: Stroke your hair.

JOMAPHIE:	Have you not felt it?
NGANGA JUAM PARFAIT MAPITY:	And when she is not here, she sits like a 375 potter, shaping your future between her palms, striking together stones to make the sparks for your eyes.
CHERUBIN:	A child in need draws a mother to her side.
JOMAPHIE:	As blood draws the shark. As bare feet 380 draw the vampire bat.
NGANGA JUAM PARFAIT MAPITY:	The Dead, the Unborn: we come and go as we please, you know.
COLLY:	What, even now the dog's bust?
ANORAX:	Yeah, how will you get back now? Now 385 Kozo's broken.
MUDASHIMWA:	*(Amused)* What? Do you think we need a wooden carving to carry us? – Ha ha! 'Fetch, Kozo!' 'Kozo fetch!'
CHERUBIN:	Are we dead birds to be fetched and 390 carried in the jaws of a dog?!
MAYIFA:	Stupid also! No respect, and stupid as mud!
NGANGA JUAM PARFAIT MAPITY:	Kozo did not fetch us here! Your little sister's kindness did that. Kozo carries only – what? – flutters of longing between the three 395 realms. Kongo dead, Kongo unborn, Kongo living.
MAYIFA:	No one say to us 'Do this. Do that'. Not government, not foreigners. None.
MUDASHIMWA:	We go where curiosity takes us. 400
CHERUBIN:	And love, of course.
JOMAPHIE:	And chocolate, sometimes.
OBI:	I'm sorry Liam broke it, all the same.

ANORAX:	We never stole it in the first place, you know? We aren't missionaries or slavers or 405 archaeologists or anything heavy like that!
NGANGA JUAM PARFAIT MAPITY:	*(With heavy irony)* You astound me.
WHITMAN:	Not the descendants of, Anorax means. We only stole Kozo from the museum.
ROCHENDA:	I stole Kozo from the museum, he means. 410
HARRY:	Whitman means, we aren't the people who nicked it from you, way back.
MUDASHIMWA:	But it was not stolen. You thought it was stolen?
CHERUBIN:	The Nganga sold it. To a collector. 415
	Mayifa chunters discontentedly; clearly she disapproved.
JOMAPHIE:	I believe the year was 1900.
NGANGA JUAM PARFAIT MAPITY:	The village had need of a well, and wells cost money. One must be practical in this life – and out of this life, come to that … But I am anxious for the boy, Liam. Wife? 420
MAYIFA:	*(Eventually, grudgingly snarls a suggestion)* Palm frond.
JOMAPHIE:	Ah yes! A palm frond at the door of the house! Where a house is blessed with a palm frond, no one molests a newborn child.
NGANGA JUAM PARFAIT MAPITY:	I am tempted to ask, who would do so 425 anyway? … But you are right, boy. Your museum may rightly be angered by the damage. They paid fully £5 for the nkisi in 1900.

ANORAX:	We'll explain to them. 430
	The visitors laugh out loud.
MUDASHIMWA:	You can try.
HARRY:	What d'you mean?
GROGS:	He's going to wipe our minds when he goes, that's what! So we don't remember anything! That's what happened to Matt 435 Damon in *Mindwash*.
NGANGA JUAM PARFAIT MAPITY:	No need. With young people we are safe to show ourselves. If they speak of it afterwards, they are never believed.
AJAX:	But it's like proof, innit. That odd stuff 440 happens. It's important.
OBI:	**Paranormal**. All that.
CHERUBIN:	If you were to say …
JOMAPHIE:	… 'Last night we were visited by the Countrymen of the Dead' … 445
MUDASHIMWA:	… they would say you had been chewing bark.
AJAX:	Bark?
KELLY:	Barking mad, he means.
HARRY:	Or barking up the wrong tree. 450
MUDASHIMWA:	Actually, I meant chewing bark for the sake of its mind-altering properties.
GROGS:	Wha'?
HARRY:	Off our faces, he means.
KELLY:	Loved up. 455
OBI:	High.

| NGANGA JUAM PARFAIT MAPITY: | Quaint **vernacular** aside – you would not be believed. Young people never are. |

The ghosts get up, preparing to leave.

CHERUBIN:	*(Leaving)* Unjust, but true.
HARRY:	Shame. The newspapers would love it. 460
ANORAX:	We could always post it on the Internet!
MUDASHIMWA:	*(Holding the wardrobe door open for Jomaphie)* In that case you would most certainly be disbelieved. One more lie among so many!

Mudashimwa leaves by the window.

The witch Mayifa makes a big song and dance of squeezing herself back under the bed, glaring and glowering at them. She appears not to fit, and rummages in her clothing to pull out a lump of palm tree to make it easier. She exits.

NGANGA JUAM PARFAIT MAPITY:	*(Privately to Rochenda, downstage)* **Sois calme**, child. The loss of a mother is as when a 465 mountain rises up beneath your hearth. It spills hot ashes over you, and scalding porridge. It tears the walls of your house apart. Everything gets broken. As time passes, and you grow bigger … 470
ROCHENDA:	… Don't tell me. 'Time's a great healer.' That's what they all say. 'Time heals everything.'
NGANGA JUAM PARFAIT MAPITY:	Oh no! How can it? The mountain does not go away. It remains there – a mountain in 475 the wrong place. But as you look back from afar, it comes to seem smaller in the landscape. Smaller. Death is not spiteful, you

know. It has no malice. It is not some
grinning enemy. It is simply a mountain; a   480
big, stony mountain. It should not be there,
but *(Shrugs)* who can move mountains? Best
to think of the view from the top and your
mother watching you from up there.
Through very powerful binoculars. *Sois*   485
calme, **ma chère**.

OBI: Sorry again about Kozo.

NGANGA JUAM
PARFAIT MAPITY: *(He shrugs, and says as he exits via the*
washbasket) To make a new nkisi takes only a
lump of wood and a chisel.

Exit all ghosts. Liam enters. He is carrying a rabbit,
a tortoise, bird in a cage. He is beside himself,
breathless from running.

Scene 2

Rochenda's bedroom.

LIAM: I brought what I could! There's no goats.
Who has goats? But I got— Where are they?
Have they gone? You never let them go?!

KELLY: What on earth?

LIAM: Well, where was I going to get a goat?   5

GROGS: Why did you want one?

AJAX: To put the magic back in the dog, 'course.

FILLY: But he smashed it to pieces! Now he wants
to mend it?

LIAM:	I wasn't trying to smash it! I was trying to 10 take it back! I have to take it back!
WHITMAN:	Too right, you do. That's someone's rabbit! You don't own a rabbit.
ROCHENDA:	He means the curse. You don't have to take back the curse, Liam. You never sent a 15 curse. The dog's got no magic.
LIAM:	That's rubbish. It brought the coins, didn't it? It brought the ghosts!
OBI:	He's not wrong. Kozo's done plenty magic since the museum. Those coins didn't get 20 here by themselves.
ROCHENDA:	Yes, but our messages didn't go! Kozo doesn't believe in us, because we're not Kongo. It didn't go, Liam.
ANORAX:	And the dog doesn't DO wishes. Why does 25 no one believe me?
LIAM:	Shove that. Shove you and your lame excuses. I KNOW it worked.

He draws Rochenda aside.

LIAM:	It's just like he said. It wasn't a message. It wasn't a wish. I willed it, Roche. I willed it. 30 It was in my head – this thing, this hate. Like he said: not words. Way past words. *(He slaps* *at his head)* Like a nail in here and someone banging it in. And then I hammered it into the dog and I KNOW it 35 went because it was gone out of here. It was. 'Cos then when Mum got ill, I couldn't remember a single reason why I'd hate a baby. Because all the hate was gone out of

my head and the dog had it. So I've got to 40
get it back. I've got to take it back, that curse,
or Mum's going to die and the baby's going
to die and it'll be my fault ... Where's the
dog?

ROCHENDA: What d'you mean? Oh! It was just ... er ... 45
Where's the dog, guys?

HARRY: Did they take it with them?

JOJO: I hope so.

COLLY: I don't think so.

LIAM: But I fetched these – to pay the penalty! To 50
make it right with the nganga! Where's the
ruddy dog?

OBI: Liam, it doesn't matter. It's a Kongo thing.
There isn't any magic unless you're Kongo.
We just got a glimpse ... 55

LIAM: What, you think Rochenda's little sister is
Kongo? It worked for her!

KELLY: She believed in it. Absolutely. Little children
can do that.

LIAM: I CAN DO IT! But now there's no dog, 60
dammit!

FILLY: We'll get him back, Liam. We will. We'll get
him back.

OBI: Don't tell him that!

JOJO: You shouldn't make promises you can't 65
keep, Filly.

HARRY: Added to which, he's off his tree! You
shouldn't go encouraging him.

FILLY:	The chief said anyone could make a new one with a lump of a wood and a chisel. 70
LIAM:	He did? Really?
COLLY:	Did anyone bring a chisel to the sleepover? Well, there's a surprise.
FILLY:	We could still make one though, couldn't we? Jojo made a teddy bear in Textiles. 75
ANORAX:	I'll look up 'nkisi' on the Net. There might be instructions.
OBI:	Anorax, there's instructions on the Net how to cook your own eyeballs. Doesn't mean it's a good idea! 80
LIAM:	There's no time! *(He has a sudden idea)* … I could use a real dog. What's wrong with a real dog? A real dog will do!

He tries to grab Jojo's pet dog.

JOJO:	NO! Daisy's not a wishing dog! Not Daisy! She's not magic. Daisy's just stupid and 85 ordinary! Don't! Somebody! Don't let him hurt Daisy!
WHITMAN:	*(Trying to talk him down)* It wouldn't work, Liam. She's only got one mouth, look.

The boys pile in to rescue Jojo's dog.

Liam snatches up the tortoise and rabbit instead.

REST:	NO, LIAM! 90
WHITMAN:	Look, where's the second mouth on a tortoise? Give it here. You've forgotten it needs a mouth at both ends.

LIAM: But I only need one direction! I only need the Unborn! 95

WHITMAN: Well, which end's that? And a rabbit's nothing like a nkisi, look. You drive a nail into a rabbit, what have you got? A dead rabbit is all.

ANORAX: Likewise the tortoise. 100

He slips the tortoise and rabbit into a drawer and drapes a towel over the birdcage.

LIAM: A lump of wood and a chisel? Is that what he said?

WHITMAN: Show me either, and I'll give it a try.

They come up with a variety of things – ornament, rugby ball, fruit, Velcro tabs off trainers, pot pourri for inside. They assemble them into a dog, all the time saying how pointless and stupid it is.

KELLY: What do we do for mouths? Like Whit says: it has to have a mouth at each end. 105

ROCHENDA: Minnie has mittens – plasticky mittens. I'll get them.

Exit Rochenda.

OBI: *(Only to Whitman, though he is overheard)* What are we doing? This is mad.

WHITMAN: We're giving Liam a reason to come down from the ceiling, right? 110

GROGS: Speak for yourself. I'm making a Death-Dog!

ANORAX: Mass hysteria. Like I said.

WHITMAN: Catching, isn't it?

They add a joss stick and light it.

Enter Rochenda holding the mittens.

ROCHENDA: Is Minnie in here? I can't find Minnie. She's 115
not in her room. She's not downstairs.
Where's Minnie? It's four in the morning!

REST: Minnie?

*They scatter (we presume) throughout the house,
calling, and return shortly not having found her.*

AJAX: Nothing. She's nowhere.

GROGS: D'you think … 120

WHITMAN: Save the zombie suggestions.

GROGS: *(Offended)* What, you think I'm going to say
she's been eaten by zombies? Give us some
credit.

WHITMAN: Sorry, Grogs. 125

GROGS: I was just going to say, maybe the dog's
carried her off to the Country of the Dead.

REST: Grogs!?

AJAX: Or the Future.

WHITMAN: *(The voice of reason)* I really don't think the 130
dog took Minnie.

AJAX: Might have. What fetches a dog back?

HARRY: Whistling!

They try it.

JOJO: Pringles? … Chocolate! We could try
chocolate! 135

ANORAX: *(Thoughtfully logical)* No. No, chocolate brought the tribesmen, not the dog.

GROGS: Another dog?

FILLY: Is your dog on heat, Jojo?

JOJO: Daisy doesn't like all that ... Anyway. She's been spayed. 140

COLLY: *(Darkly inspired)* Or maybe THEY came back. Wanted pay-back after all. Yeah! They said they were friendly but really ... All that nicely-nicely '*sois calme, chère*'. That witch 145 was livid about us messing with a nkisi.

FILLY: She said about flesh and blood, too. You heard her. Flesh and blood. That's what they want most, 'cos it's the only way they can be alive again! 150

OBI: That's not what – as a baby, yes. She didn't mean ...

GROGS: Maybe they took Minnie, so one of them could come back to life in her place!

OBI: Not helpful, Grogs. Really not helpful. 155

KELLY: And that's why they came! Right from the start, I bet. A life for a life.

AJAX: Or they wanted a child bride, or something.

WHITMAN: Now hold on ...

COLLY: You know it makes sense, Whit. 160

Whitman takes charge.

WHITMAN: No. I don't. I don't know it makes sense. I know you're talking junk. I know that yesterday we were making dumb jokes about

dead people – Marilyn Monroe and Ghengis
Khan and Lady Godiva. Then the real   165
thing turned up, and we were – 'Waaaah! It's
the Underworld come to rip our lights out!'
Oh look, though! It turns out it's Revels and
chocolate oranges. And there's this cool man
with his 37 languages and his don't-mind-us 170
religion and his crabby wife and his mate
who does head-reading. But – hey! – the nice
nganga's no sooner out the door than he's
back to, like, the Child Catcher in *Chitty
Chitty Bang Bang* with his big net and his   175
creepy knees. Can you make your minds up
please, people? I know what I saw this
evening, and I don't think I imagined it. I
don't think any of us are clever enough to
imagine it! We're so stuff-full of stupid   180
ideas and bad movies and prehistoric – like –
'Ugg' – they should put us in a museum so
people could come and look at us and have a
laugh. Life for a life, my eye!

Into the silence that follows, a mobile phone
sounds. Liam answers it. He smiles in response to
what he hears.

LIAM: *(Talking into the phone)* Right. Great. And   185
           Mum? Great. That's great. Tell her – that's
           great … Yeah … I'm at home. Where else
           would I be? *(He rings off)* That was my step-
           dad. Mike. Mum just had a little girl. They're
           both fine. What d'you know! I got a sister!   190

Liam is warmly congratulated from all sides. There
is big relief.

ROCHENDA: I HAVEN'T!

She runs at Whitman and beats on him with her fists (as if hammering nails into him).

ROCHENDA: MINNIEEEEE! WHERE'S MINNIE!

He shields himself with their sorry-looking model dog so she hammers on that as well.

ROCHENDA: WHERE'S MINNIE, MUM? MUM? FIND HER, MUM! FIND HER! I'M SORRY. I SHOULD'VE LOOKED AFTER HER! YOU SEE HOW IT   195 IS, MUM? I CAN'T DO IT. I TOLD YOU: I CAN'T DO IT ANY MORE! IT'S NO GOOD! PLEEEEASE!

*There is an **ominous** thump thump thump on the stairs; a noise that might be any one of their worst imaginings.*

JOJO: Something's coming!

The door handle blips.

GROGS: Don't let it in! Put a chair against the door!   200 Don't let it get in!

They do, but Minnie pushes her way in anyway, with Kozo on a string, bumping him along the ground.

ROCHENDA: *(As if holding her breath)* Where have you been, Min?

MINNIE: Walking my doggie. I took Kozo for a walk.

REST: YES!   205

ROCHENDA: At four in the morning?

MINNIE: Dogs can see in the dark. Didn't you know?

There is a general tendency to dance.

KELLY: *(To Minnie)* Time someone was in bed.

ROCHENDA: Yes. Come on, Min. Let's tuck you up. If you don't get to bed soon it will be time to get up. *(To Whitman)* Sorry, Whit. 210

WHITMAN: Don't mention it. At least you didn't use rusty nails and a hammer. *(Holding up the home-made dog)* … And look, it still worked without them. 215

Exit Rochenda, Kelly and Minnie.

JOJO: Daisy wants to go home now.

FILLY: She's not the only one. It's daylight almost.

ANORAX: *(To Whitman, about the dancing)* Bit tribal for me.

WHITMAN: You and me both.

They withdraw to a safe distance.

WHITMAN: Someone's going to have to take that back to the museum. 220

ANORAX: What, Kozo?

WHITMAN: And it's not going to be me. Look at it. It looks like road-kill.

ANORAX: We could leave it on the doorstep – leave a note saying it was abducted by aliens. 225

WHITMAN: That's no way to talk about your mates …

ANORAX: What's that in its mouth?

Whitman sidles over to the nkisi, takes a furtive look and sidles back.

WHITMAN: If you swear not to tell … I'd say it's a palm
frond.   230

ANORAX: What, like the witch …? Put it by the baby's
front door – all that?

WHITMAN: Mmm. Life insurance, Kongo-style.

ANORAX: Where …? That's … How?

WHITMAN: One hairy mystery.   235

ANORAX: Hairier than the Yeti!

WHITMAN: Fancy a trip over to Liam's house tomorrow?
A pound says you can't plant that palm frond
beside his door without the neighbours
spotting you and sending for the police.   240

ANORAX: I don't even know where he lives.

WHITMAN: Let's find out, then.

*They move over to Liam. Each puts an arm round
his shoulders as if casual mates, with the aim of
getting his address out of him. Whitman pockets
the palm frond.*

Exit all, in ones and twos.

*Enter Rochenda. Alone now, she picks up the
homemade nkisi lying discarded on the floor, and
sits on the bed with it. Without cause, the hair
clipped up on top of her head comes unfastened
and falls over her shoulders.*

ROCHENDA: *(Calmly)* Mum?

The End

Glossary

artefact something man-made, such as a tool

assagai a light spear made of wood used by certain African tribes

bona fide genuine

ceremonially during a formal (often religious) occasion

Chanel no. 5 an expensive, famous perfume

colonisation when one country takes control of another country

concatenating fusing together

cornucopia a goat's horn used as a container

credibility something that can be believed

cut and shut the illegal practice of welding together the bodies of two cars damaged in road accidents

divines senses

droning continuous dull noise

Elim pentecostal a Christian church

essences concentrated parts of a substance

fakir a holy man

forger someone who makes fake items with the aim of selling them as if they were genuine

Freud an Austrian psychologist (1856–1939) who believed he could explain why people behave the way they do

furtive secretive

impelled moved

implication something that is implied or suggested

joss stick a stick made of incense

Jungian after Carl Jung (1875–1961), a famous Swiss psychologist

loincloths strips of cloth worn around the lower body

ma chère French for 'my dear'

mots justes French phrase meaning 'I couldn't have put it better myself'

nganga local wise man

nkisi a sacred artefact

numismatic coin collecting

Oedipus complex one of Freud's theories

ominous threatening
orenda spiritual force
Pagans followers of the Pagan religion
paranormal something that cannot be explained by science
reincarnation a belief that when a person dies, their soul moves
    into another body
serene calm
shabby-chic second-hand but still stylish
sois calme French for 'calm down'
sois gentille French for 'be nice'
superstition a belief not based on reason
SWAT stands for Special Weapons and Tactics
terrapins small freshwater turtles
vernacular everyday language
voodoo a religious cult associated with witchcraft
whyfor reason

Activities

Activity 1: Pre-reading

Before you begin

> In this activity, you will make some predictions about the play before you read it and decide what questions you would like answered.

1   **Work on your own.** Look carefully at the front cover of the play. Create a mind map with 'Fetch!' in the centre. Around it, map everything you think it might be about.

2   **Work on your own.** List six questions you would like answered about the play, using the words 'who', 'what', 'when', 'where', 'why' and 'how'. After you have read Act One Scene 1, look again at these questions to see how many have been answered.

3   **Work with a partner.** Discuss what you predict the play will be about. Together, come up with a 'blurb' for the play that hints at your predictions and that makes the play sound exciting for a reader your age.

4   **Work in a group.** Read the information in the character list. Revisit all your mind maps and discuss how your character knowledge might change some of your original predictions.

Activity 2: Research

Act One Scene 1

In this activity, you will consider the differences in the language used by the students and the Curator, and complete some research about Kongolese culture.

1   **Work on your own.** Read Act One Scene 1. List all the words that relate to Kongo culture (e.g. *Assagai*). Write a clear definition of each word using the Curator's explanations to help you. Then compare your definitions to those in the glossary. Which definitions are clearer?

2   **Work on your own.** List the ways in which the language of the Curator is different from that of the students. Find examples of differences in vocabulary, formality and clarity. Try to give reasons for the differences you find.

3   **Work with a partner.** Share your differences. Then make a list of any similar ways in which your own language differs from that of your teachers and other adults.

4   **Work in a group.** Produce an A4 information sheet entitled 'Kongo Minkisi' (plural of Nkisi). Include detailed information about different types of Minkisi and how they are believed to work. Use the Internet, the library and any other available resources to help you.

Activity 3: Rochenda and Minnie

Act One Scene 2

In this activity, you will explore the relationship between Rochenda and her sister, Minnie.

1 **Work on your own.** Read Act One Scene 2. List all the moments in the scene where Rochenda says something negative to Minnie (e.g. *no*, *don't*).

2 **Work on your own.** For each moment you have listed, try to explain how Rochenda and Minnie feel. Turn your list into a table that looks like this

Example	How Rochenda feels	How Minnie feels
Don't touch it, Minnie (line 1, page 7)	Protective of Kozo.	Curious about Kozo.

3 **Work with a partner.** Take one character each and practise reading the scene from *Don't touch it* to *Swallow a nail and die* (lines 1–33, pages 7-8). Use the ideas from your table to help you decide how to read each line.

Now swap roles. Did you read the part in the same way as your partner? List any differences, including the reasons why.

Activity 4: What comes next?

Act One Scene 3

In this activity, you will make some predictions about the events in this scene based on your reading of the play to this point.

1 **Work on your own.** Read Act One Scene 3. Then copy and complete the table below to show which characters think the nkisi is magic. Find evidence from this and previous scenes to support your opinion.

Character	Believe in the nkisi?	Evidence
Obi	No	*You're never talking magic, man?* (lines 64–65, page 15)

2 **Work on your own.** Using your evidence from Question 1, select two characters with different opinions on the nkisi. Script a conversation between them in which they argue about Kozo and try to justify their opinions.

3 **Work with a partner.** Practise a dramatic reading of the scene you have just scripted. Make suggestions to your partner for any changes they might make, and any stage directions they could add.

4 **Work in a group.** Improvise the next scene, which shows what the group ends up doing with their discovery.

Activity 5: Modes of Address

Act One Scene 4

In this activity, you will consider the way we address different people and what effect this has.

1   **Work on your own.** Count the number of times Liam uses the word 'Sir' in this short scene. Why does he do this and what effect does it have?

2   **Work on your own.** Make two lists. One should contain respectful addresses to adults, and the other should show how you address your friends.

Address to adults	Address to friends
Sir	Mate

3   **Work with a partner.** Read through the scene, replacing the word 'sir' with other options from your list. List the different effects you think they would have on the Curator.

4   **Work with a partner.** Take on the roles of Liam and the Curator. The Curator begins with the coin and Liam has 3 minutes to use all of his persuasive skills to get the Curator to return it. Consider the most effective addresses you could use.

Activity 6: Hot seating History

Act One Scene 5

In this activity, you will select information from the text. Use it to produce a detailed drawing and to hot seat your partner.

1 **Work on your own.** Draw a picture of the coin using all of the details from this scene. Annotate your drawing with everything you have added from the text.

2 **Work on your own.** List all the famous figures mentioned in the scene. Separate them into two categories: 'Historical' and 'Imaginary'.

3 **Work on your own.** Look at your list of 'Historical' figures. Write down what you think each one is known for. Then write three questions you would like to ask them.

4 **Work with a partner.** Take on the roles of the historical characters mentioned in the scene and hot seat one another, using the questions you have written.

Activity 7: Flashback to tragedy

Act One Scene 6

In this activity, you will write an additional 'flashback' scene in the play where some of Rochenda's friends discuss her mother's death and how she is coping.

1   **Work on your own.** Read Act One Scene 6, and think about Filly's line just before Minnie enters, when she mentions Rochenda's mother's death.

2   **Work with a partner.** Choose four characters from the play. Make some notes about how they might respond and react to the death of Rochenda's mother.

3   **Work on your own.** Use the notes from Question 2 to create a 'flashback' scene of the day after Rochenda's mother's death, where the four characters meet and interact. Use a playscript format, and try to convey how each of your chosen characters respond in ways that match their personality in the play. This should be a serious, dramatic scene, so make sure your script is sensitive and mature.

Activity 8: Being Liam

Act One Scene 7

> In this activity, you will explore Liam's motivations for sending the message through the nkisi. By writing in role, you will show empathy with Liam's character.

1 **Work on your own.** Read Act One Scene 7, focusing your attention on Liam's monologue or message through the nkisi (lines 25–38, page 26). Try to imagine the anger and bitterness he is feeling to want to convey such a message.

2 **Work with a partner.** Practise delivering the monologue to each other, trying to show Liam's inner feelings and frustrations through pitch, pace, volume and tone. Support each other by offering feedback and advice.

3 **Work on your own.** Write four sentences to explain why Liam feels the way he does about his soon-to-be-born sibling. The sentences should show your understanding of his inner torment and anger.

4 **Work on your own.** Imagine you are Liam and have just sent the message through the nkisi. Express your thoughts, feelings and emotions in a diary extract or sequence of blogs.

Activity 9: Terror and aftermath

Act One Scenes 8 and 9

> In this activity, you will explore how the different characters respond to Rochenda's retelling of the apparitions the night before. You will then show your understanding by writing in role as one of the characters, expressing their thoughts and feelings about the night's occurrences.

1 **Work on your own.** Read Act One Scene 8. Imagine how this would be conveyed on stage. Write two sentences to explain how Rochenda might have felt.

2 **Work on your own.** Read Act One Scene 9. Make brief notes about how each character responds differently to Rochenda's account.

3 **Work with a partner.** Discuss the ways in which the characters' responses are different, and log your ideas in a table like the one below.

Character	Quote	What this shows
Kelly	*Does she look as if she dreamed it?* (line 7, page 29)	She is more caring and protective of her best friend, and is willing to believe her.
Colly	*You dreamed it* (line 218, page 36)	

4 **Work on your own.** Choose a character who has heard Rochenda's recount. Write their blog or diary entry expressing thoughts and feelings about the 'story', and how they feel about the nkisi. Use your imagination, but draw on your knowledge of your chosen character.

Activity 10: Performance Advice

Act One Scene 10

> In this activity, you will be giving advice to some young actors preparing to play the characters in 'Fetch!' in a stage production.

1 **Work on your own.** Read Act One Scene 10. As you read, consider how the different characters respond to the 'ghost-watch' events, and especially the re-appearance of the apparitions.

2 **Work on your own.** Complete a table like the one below to gather notes on how Liam, Rochenda and two other characters of your choice respond and react towards the end of this scene.

Character	Reactions
Liam	Eager to meet and talk with the apparitions. Seems desperate to undo any harm he may have done through his 'message' …
Rochenda	

3 **Work with a partner.** Share your notes and discuss any differences. Agree on three characters, then write advice for actors playing these characters in this particular scene. Focus on what the character is like, the way they respond to the apparitions, and how this might be conveyed on stage through voice, facial expression and movement.

Activity 11: The Waiting Place

Act Two Scene 1

In this activity, you will focus on your powers of description and your ability to imagine strange new places.

1 **Work on your own.** Read Act Two Scene 1. Whenever a character mentions 'The Waiting Hall', imagine what this 'place' might be like and how it might feel to be there as you wait to begin a new life journey.

2 **Work with a partner.** Without conferring, draw a representation of the 'Waiting Place'. This is an imaginative task, and there is no single 'correct' way to see this strange place. Swap drawings, then discuss similarities and differences and why you each made certain choices.

3 **Work on your own.** Add descriptive words and phrases around your drawing. These will form a 'palette' of useful language excerpts for you to construct the piece of writing below.

4 **Work on your own.** Using your drawing and 'palette', write a description of the 'Waiting Place' and how it feels to be there. This might be most effective in first person narrative voice (e.g.: 'I looked around me ...'), but you can use third person if you prefer. Try to use language choices to impact on the reader and convey the otherworldly atmosphere.

Activity 12: Fetch! 2

Act Two Scene 2

> In this activity, you will think of ways to continue the story and characters from the play in a 'sequel', and write a short opening scene from your idea for *Fetch! 2*.

1 **Work on your own.** Read Act Two Scene 2. Start to think about the different ways the play could continue. What might happen to the different characters next?

2 **Work with a partner.** Copy and complete this table to outline how the characters in Scene 2 have changed by the end of the play. This will help you to decide who you might include in your 'sequel'.

Character	Start of play	End of play
Liam	Grief and anger at mother's relationship with stepfather.	Is more at peace, and happy he has a new sister.
Rochenda	On the verge of despair because of her mother's recent death.	

3 **Work on your own.** Write a brief summary of your 'sequel' idea, explaining what will happen and which characters from the original will be in your follow-up.

4 **Work on your own.** Write the first short scene from your sequel. Use playscript format, and try to write in the same style and approach as the author. Make sure your dialogue matches the way the characters talk in the original play!

Activity 13: Review

After reading

In this activity, you will write a review of a 'performance' of the play
Fetch!, imagining a popular local newspaper is reporting.

1 **Work on your own.** After reading the play, list the key events that
occur. This will help you to summarise the story of the play, which
will be an important part of your review.

2 **Work with a partner.** List the main characters. Next to each name,
write a short description of their personality and how an audience
might respond to them.

3 **Work in a group.** Imagine there has been a school performance of
the play and the local press have been there. Agree on three
positive comments they might make about the play and
performance, and three things they may criticise or feel were less
effective. Write these as a list.

4 **Work on your own.** It's time to write your review. Start with a brief
outline of the plot or story (but don't give away too much!). Then
evaluate what was good about the play in performance and what
was less effective. Remember that this is a newspaper review and
will be written in an entertaining style; it wouldn't be too critical
of a school performance!